Book 2 in The Yoga Mat
Cozy Mystery Series

Goddess, Guilted

By Jacqueline M. Green

Other books in The Yoga Mat Cozy Mystery Series:

Book 1: *Corpse Pose, Indeed*

Book 2: *Goddess, Guilted*

Book 3: *Warrior, Well Dead (due in October 2019)*

Chapter 1

Seated on my yoga mat at the front of the room, I inhaled deeply and silently counted dollar bills instead of breaths. How much money had this class would brought in? Several students had bought passes and a few had paid the drop-in rate. I shook my shoulders to relax them and opened my eyes. My students stared at me, waiting.

Apparently, centering time had gone on a touch too long.

Oops.

I gave my best yoga instructor smile and lifted my hands over my head, beginning the class.

Money worries played a huge distraction these days as my fledgling yoga studio struggled to bounce back from last month's drop. Apparently, students are hesitant to try a new studio where someone died during *savasana*, particularly if that student was murdered. My little studio, The Yoga Mat, located on Main Street in downtown Jasper, wasn't booming.

Yet, I told myself. It wasn't booming *yet*.

I pushed aside my worries as I took the class onto their knees for warm-up Cat and Cow poses then to standing to begin a vinyasa flow. Today our flow focused on the Goddess Pose in preparation for a visit from the "goddess." At least that's what she calls herself: Goddess Tamara, Yogi to the Stars.

The first time I heard of her, my eyes rolled involuntarily. However, Tamara is the yoga flavor of the month as she instructs everyone who is anyone on the yoga lifestyle. She has appeared on the covers of yoga magazines as well celebrity and women's magazines.

A series of events led to Tamara's workshop at The Yoga Mat. First, Angelica, the younger sister of my friend Josie, began to work for Tamara in Los Angeles. Then Josie's brother began to date her. With two such "ins" with the goddess herself, well, of course I had to see if she would teach a workshop at The Yoga Mat.

She graciously agreed – for an outrageous fee. Fortunately, we had quickly filled the roster, attracting students from surrounding towns and even as far away as Sacramento to the three-hour workshop, *The Goddess in You: How Yoga Can Turn Anyone into a Goddess.*

I wasn't breathing easy just yet, however. This workshop would need to deliver the goods or the reputation of The Yoga Mat would suffer. With my nearly new studio, I couldn't afford more negative publicity.

Stormy McMaster, my part-time receptionist and full-time shadow, said the phone still rang off the hook during the day with people wanting to be put on the waiting list. If this workshop was a success, I would try to bring in more celebrity teachers. But right now,

I wanted to be done with the glitz and glamor of the "Goddess" as soon as possible. The most I wanted to worry about was my little studio and the monthly Jaspar Movie Night and Silent Auction.

It hadn't been so quiet last month, when a student had died in my class and I had been accused of poisoning her. It still grates, but I work every day at not being bitter.

Sometimes, I'm more successful at it than others.

Today, I smirked a little – no, I'm not proud of it – as I watched Detective Neil Samuelson fall out of Goddess pose just as I brought everyone into a balancing variation by lifting their heels. Neil had tried to make up for arresting me last month by buying a six-month pass to my studio. It took more than that for me to forgive him, however, even if those blue-gray eyes of his were mesmerizing. *Ahem. Not that I noticed.*

I pulled my eyes from the buff detective and scanned the room, my heart welling up with gratitude. My sister, Cindy, was in her usual place near the door. Not only was she one of my part-time yoga instructors, she was also the county sheriff. Next to her was my best friend, CeCe.

Angelica was near the front of the room and followed my cues easily into Triangle and then a high lunge. Angelica had accompanied her boss and brother back to Jasper for several days of relaxation in addition to the workshop.

When class was over and students were milling around the lobby and pulling on their shoes, I ducked into my small office to take a payment. My sister stuck her head in the door.

"We're going for pizza. You in?"

"Pizza? Seriously?" I handed back my student's credit card, then paused to stare at Cindy. "You just gave your body this enormous treat, this gift of yoga for an hour, and now you want to go and spoil it with pizza?"

"So, you're not coming?"

"Oh, no, I'm in. I'm starving." I grinned as she shook her head, her blond ponytail bobbing back and forth. "Give me a few minutes to close and I'll meet you there."

It took longer than usual to close up for the night. Students wanted to stay and chat excitedly about Goddess Tamara's upcoming workshop.

"I saw her once in Orange County and she was just so ethereal," one woman said. "She really spoke to the mind-body connection."

Like I do every day. I gritted my teeth and took a deep calming breath through my nose. Stormy, standing next to me, must have heard my breath because she threw me a smirk and then moved to tidy the studio. I made a face at her, then looked calmly back at my students. They were excited about someone famous coming in, that was all. Not to be crass, but if it kept them buying passes at The Yoga Mat, I was all for it.

Angelica sat quietly in an empty space in the corner, reaching a tattooed arm toward the cubbies and pulling on pink-and-purple tennis shoes. Most people who work for someone famous might be tempted to name-drop in a crowd of fans, but Angelica seemed content to listen to the chatter about her boss, Tamara. As she pressed her foot into a shoe, I tapped her shoulder.

"Josie's going to meet us at Luigi's. Do you want to join us?"

Angelica smiled shyly and nodded. "That would be great. I'm pretty hungry after that workout."

Stormy and I finally moved the chattering students out the door and we fled with Angelica down the street to Luigi's Pizzeria.

Luigi's was a classic pizza joint with red-checked tablecloths and pitchers of beer. The current owner, Lou, was the son of the original Luigi. Most nights, the place bustled with locals and tonight was no exception. I looked around the room, waving to a few people I knew.

Jennifer Parks from the Safety Blanket nonprofit waved back. She put her fingers to her ears in the international sign for "call me." I nodded and she turned back to her dinner companion, whom I noticed was Maya Anderson, the reporter at the local weekly newspaper. We were planning to do another fund-raiser for Safety Blanket and I needed to follow up with both women about it. I added "Safety Blanket" to my mental checklist.

Cindy had already ordered the pizza along with a pitcher of root beer.

"Good class tonight, sis." Cindy handed me two glasses of root beer, which I passed to Angelica and Stormy, then I accepted the next one. Neil and CeCe chimed in from their places around the table.

"Yeah, but why do we keep doing Goddess?"

"It's haaarrrd," CeCe whined.

I lifted my icy root beer glass to them. "Here's to you for doing just as much as you can do without comparing yourself to anyone else."

"Ugh. I hate it when you go all yoga teacher zen." CeCe made a face at me.

Setting down the glass, I raised my arms over my head in a big stretch. Another long day. Pizza made the perfect ending.

The owner of Luigi's Pizzeria, Lou, had just set down three large pizzas when Josie walked in, trailed by a small crowd that seemed to include family and friends as well as a woman who walked as if floating on air. Even if I hadn't already met her this week when she dropped by to check out the studio, I would have recognized the Goddess Tamara.

This being a small town, people stopped talking to stare. Josie ignored the sudden change in voices, making a beeline for our table as soon as she spotted us. A slight smile appeared on the Goddess' face as she followed Josie toward us.

"Mariah, so lovely to see you again. I am so looking forward to our workshop next weekend." She gently clasped one of my hands in both of hers. She held my hand slightly longer than necessary. I started to pull them away and noticed she turned and smiled off to the side. I followed her gaze and frowned.

Maya Anderson, the reporter, lowered her smart phone and gave me a thumbs-up. Man, she had made it across the room quickly. Tamara turned her attention back to me. "The press is always around, right?" She shrugged a delicate "what can you do?" sign.

Tamara's thin frame looked fragile until you noticed the muscles in her arms, strength built up from hours of Ashtanga yoga. I glanced down at my own slightly pudgy body, then stood a little straighter as I felt those old feelings of inadequacy try to slip in. I shook my head and reminded myself that yoga had made me both resilient and strong under that soft coating. I didn't need to compare myself to the Goddess Tamara.

"We are so happy —" I started to say before a familiar voice interrupted.

`'"Hey, don't take that. I want another." The voice rose suddenly above the throng from the corner of the restaurant. "Hey!"

I looked up and recognized Jerry McIntyre, the owner of the Corner Mercantile shop on Main Street, just as he grabbed the young waitress' arm. Startled, she jerked away and dropped the mug in her hand. Leftover beer dashed everywhere, including on Lou as he approached. He stepped between Jerry and the girl, motioning her back toward the counter.

The place went silent as Lou lowered his voice. "It's time for something else."

He reached an open hand toward his left. A server shoved a mug of what looked like soda into it. Lou swung it back around toward Jerry.

"Here you go, friend. Let's settle down with some good old Coca-Cola."

Jerry knocked the glass with his hand. Whether he did it from lack of muscle control or on purpose was hard to tell. Cindy and Neil stood up on opposite sides of our table and quietly started toward Jerry and Lou.

Cindy turned briefly back to the table. "Nothing to see here, folks. Get back to your pizza."

I dutifully picked up my slice of vegetarian pizza, but my eyes stayed on the show in the corner.

Neil slipped into position behind Lou.

"Gimme a beer – and I'm not your friend." He lifted his eyes squinting them to focus on Lou. "I know what you've been doing with my wife."

Lou took a deep breath and placed the soda glass in front of Jerry. "No more beer for you tonight, Jerry. You're cut off."

The front door swung open. Sandy McIntyre flung herself in as if the wind had blown her through the door.

Disgust fleeting across her lined face, Sandy placed her hand on her husband's shoulder but turned her attention to Lou. Her expression softened as she looked into his eyes. "I'm sorry. I didn't know where he had gotten off to tonight. We were busy unloading the truck."

Lou's eyes locked into hers as he smiled. "Don't worry about it. We've got a full house and I just don't have the patience to deal with him tonight."

Sandy turned her attention back to Jerry. She leaned in to talk softly to him, then gently nudged him up out of his seat. She noticed Maya standing nearby, her camera phone at the ready. "You didn't take any pictures of that, did you?" Maya shook her head. "You better not. He's a private citizen. You leave him alone."

"I just wanted a beer," Jerry mumbled as they stumbled toward the door.

"I know, honey." Sandy's voice changed back to soothing, which seemed to calm him down. Neil followed them out the door and stood talking to Sandy for a few moments outside.

The whole pizza shop had seemed enthralled with the drama in front of us. Tamara's eyes were wide. Jennifer sat with one hand over her mouth as she watched Sandy and Jerry leave. Maya tucked her phone into her back pocket and returned to her table.

Cindy turned back to the restaurant. "Show's over, folks. If you don't get back to eating your pizza, then I will." With that, she rejoined our table, sitting down and picking up her slice of pepperoni and sausage.

Josie and her family quickly filled in the empty spaces at the table in a chaotic scramble, Josie scooting in next to me. She grabbed a slice from the pan as I bit into the pizza, enjoying the gooey cheese stretching between my mouth and the slice.

Neil quietly slipped back into his chair across from me. He leaned across the table to say something I couldn't hear to Cindy, who nodded. "We'll follow up later," she said.

Neil nodded in response and bit into his pizza. He quietly sat and ate, then glanced up and smiled into my eyes. Oh, yes, I definitely smiled back.

Tamara kept glancing over her shoulder toward the door.

"Everything okay, Tamara?" Neil asked, putting an emphasis on the "Tam."

She jumped as if she hadn't been aware she was being watched. She nodded and picked up her water cup to sip, then paused and looked at him.

"Actually, it's pronounced Ta-MAR-uh, not TAM-ara."

Neil swallowed quickly. "I'm sorry. I didn't mean to mispronounce your name."

She waved a hand. "That's all right. It happens a lot." She glanced again over her shoulder at the door.

"I understand you used to visit Jasper when you were a child." Neil wiped his mouth, then took another bite.

Tamara avoided his eyes as she played with the water drips on the side of the frosty glass, opening her mouth to speak, then closing it again. She seemed to be weighing just what to say.

The silence started to drag out. Neil calmly leaned forward to take a bite of the garlic chicken pizza, letting the oil drip onto his plate and a drop ran down his chin.

Our eyes met over the table. I handed him a napkin. Amusement lit his eyes as he wiped off the grease, his eyes never leaving mine.

I had nearly forgotten Neil had asked the question when Tamara finally spoke.

"To answer your question, yes, we came here when I was a child. I have lots of good memories of Jasper."

"What's your favorite memory?" Neil pressed on. I could tell he was trying to make her feel more comfortable after that disturbing scene with Jerry. He watched Tamara, one eyebrow lifted quizzically. She turned to favor him with a smile.

"Detective, I couldn't even count all the good times we had here. We loved to go hiking and horseback riding when we were here, and when I got older, why, swimming at the river, right?"

Everyone except me laughed, including Tamara, whose laugh sounded like a tinkling bell. I looked around the table, then leaned toward Josie. "What's so funny?"

Josie smiled. "When we were in high school 'swimming at the river' was code for making out with a boyfriend or girlfriend."

"Ah, you had a summertime romance?" CeCe smiled. "Sounds perfect."

Tamara laughed, then reached for a slice of the vegetarian pizza. "I was only fourteen, so I don't know how perfect it was, but it was fun while it lasted."

CeCe leaned toward Tamara, her eyes dancing with mischief. "Who was this teenage Romeo?"

Tamara smiled and nudged Deangelo with her elbow. He blushed.

"Deangelo, really?" Josie's surprise was palpable.

He shrugged. "What can I say? I was a hottie back in my pre-high school days."

Tamara smiled gently. "Still are."

He blushed again and gave her a quick kiss on the cheeks as she nibbled her pizza crust.

"And how did you rekindle your romance?" I couldn't tell if CeCe was being nosey or if she was just a sucker for a good romantic tale.

Tamara and Deangelo exchanged a look. She nodded almost imperceptibly. Deangelo took a breath and squared his shoulders. "I was working in LA, see, when Angel – my sister, Angelica there – called me up and said I'd never guess who she was working for."

"He guessed like five people I had never heard of before I told him to shut up, that it was just a rhetorical question." Angelica broke in, shaking her head. "I told him, no, it's Tamara! I had run into her at the hospital where I was doing some EMT practicums and she was teaching yoga."

"Eventually, Tamara hired Angel, and Angel called me." Deangelo stopped and took a bite of his pizza as if that was the end of the story. Tamara looked at him in surprise.

"You're not going to tell the rest?"

Deangelo laughed, making it hard for him to swallow. "Nah, it makes me look like a stalker."

"You were a stalker!" Tamara and Angelica said it together.

Deangelo just laughed and continued. "I found out where else Tamara taught. Then I joined that gym and I just started showing up in her classes."

Tamara gave a pouty face. "He let me think he didn't know I was teaching there, that he just ran into me. When I found out the truth, I couldn't decide if I was mad or flattered."

"Apparently, flattery won?" CeCe asked.

Tamara turned her mouth down in an exaggerated frown. I sighed. Even her frowns were adorable.

"No, I was mad, but after a while, I forgave him and focused on the wonderful things we had in our relationship, so here we are." She waved her hand around the room. "I couldn't believe he wanted me to come home and meet his family, right? I had never met them when we were kids."

"I do remember *you*, Sheriff." Tamara looked toward my sister, sitting unobtrusively on the other side of CeCe. "You were a deputy then, and you gave Deangelo and me one of those speeches about getting outside and playing instead of making out in the movie theater on Sunday afternoons."

Cindy frowned and looked intently toward the pair. "Was I nice about it?"

Tamara tinkled her laugh once again. "Of course, Sheriff."

"That's not what you said at the time. I think you called her a b-"

Tamara quickly put her fingers to Deangelo's lips, then glanced back to Cindy. "Perhaps, but I was just a kid. In hindsight, you could not have been kinder."

Cindy raised her root beer glass in a silent cheer, then set it back down and looked around the pizzas to select her next piece. She grabbed one from right in front of me and waved in under my nose.

"OOOhhhh, ahhhhhh, smell that sausage, sis." Then she pulled it back and took a big bite off the triangle on the end, not easy to do when she was laughing so hard. My big sister liked to give me a hard time about being vegetarian.

Everyone laughed and Cindy held up her pizza slice and took a small bow. "I'm here every night, folks, keepin' it real."

I rolled my eyes. "A funny sheriff, that's what every small town needs."

Our eyes met, then she looked toward the door, worry flickering across her face. If you didn't know you, you might have missed it. But I could tell. She was unsettled by the scene with Jerry and Sandy.

Chapter 2

The next morning after the 9 o'clock Mamas and Me Class, I jogged down Main Street to the Corner Mercantile for a few needed studio supplies. A little bell dinged to announce my arrival as I snagged a red basket. Surprisingly, Jerry McIntyre stood fully upright and seemingly functioning at the cashier's counter, Jennifer Parks standing opposite, her hand on his arm.

They both turned when the bell dinged, Jennifer's mouth arching downward and Jerry squinting his eyes to see who it was. Jennifer leaned toward him and said something in a low voice. Jerry jerked away from her and turned to fuss with something on the counter behind them. She stared at him for a long moment, then turned toward the front door.

I gave a little quick wave to them both and hurried for the far aisle. I didn't want to get in the middle of their apparent argument. Besides, I needed to make this a quick trip and get back to the studio. We were completely and surprisingly out of tissues at The Yoga Mat. One of my students apparently had quite the cold. I tried to remember whom I had heard sniffling this week but couldn't quite identify the culprit.

Since we were nearly out of antiseptic wipes and paper towels as well, I decided to buy a couple of back-up containers. I typically bought most of my paper products during runs to the big-box stores in Sacramento, but I wasn't sure when I would make it later this week, what with Goddess Tamara's weekend workshop taking a huge chunk of my time and energy.

Besides, I liked to support local retailers. After all, karma, right? If I wanted other local businesses to support me, I needed to support them in turn. To be fair, several had dropped in for classes at the studio, although only a couple had purchased passes.

After gathering what I needed, I approached the cashier's counter that ran along the store's large front window.

"Morning, Jerry."

He looked at me as if he couldn't quite place me. His blood-shot eyes seemed remarkably focused, considering how I had seen him last. He didn't usually run the front counter and I rarely ran into him. I wasn't even sure he knew who I was.

"I'm Mariah Stevens, Jerry. Remember? I opened the yoga studio down the way about nine months ago?"

Jerry smiled and nodded. "Oh, yes, and how has the gestation period of your baby gone?" He reached for my basket and began setting my items on the counter to scan.

I gave a surprised laugh. I hadn't really considered that the first nine months could be considered a gestation period for my studio. Tilting my head to look at him, I responded. "Things do seem to be doing okay right now."

He smiled again. "Then you have assuredly set a stable foundation. Well done. First time business owner?"

I nodded and couldn't quite keep a grin off my face.

"Best of luck to you then. Owning your own business has all the ups and downs you might expect, but I wish yours great success."

I paid for my items and started out the door, mulling over the longest conversation I'd had with Jerry since I moved to town last year.

I very nearly skipped down Main Street toward The Yoga Mat. I still loved seeing the logo in the window and the lights on inside.

Wait a minute, why were the lights on inside? I was the only one teaching this morning and I had turned them off when I left.

I jerked open the door. Stormy met me with a "shh" sign, her pointer finger to her lips.

"Stormy, what is going on?"

"Mariah, shhh. The Goddess is embodying the space she'll be working in."

What the heck? I peeked over the top of the partial doors into the dimly lit studio. Tamara sat in a lotus position on a mat in the middle of the room, her eyes closed. Lotus was hard on ankle and knee joints, so I typically recommended students sit with their legs in the less-difficult crisscross or a stacked position. That, and my thighs were a little too thick to make the position comfortable. Clearly, stick-woman Tamara did not have the same body issues.

I pulled Stormy into my office. *My* office, I reminded myself. "What is she doing here? Why did you let her in?"

Stormy's shoulders drooped and she raised her hands palm up in the "I don't know" position.

"I ran into her outside the hotel and she remembered me, so she asked if she could come to" – at this, Stormy used air quotes – " 'embody' the space where she would be holding the workshop. I said I would have to check with you, and then she followed me here, like a puppy."

"Well, she can't stay. I have a class starting in twenty-five minutes."

"I told her that. I didn't know what to do. She just scooted past me into the studio. Next thing I know, she's chanting on a mat in the middle of the room." Stormy picked up the purse she had set down and looked at me pointedly. "I tried to text you, and I didn't leave her alone here."

She looked back over her shoulder as if she were afraid Tamara would pop out at her any second. "Can I go?"

I threw back my head and blew out a breath. "Yes, ya coward. Go."

Stormy smiled and blew me a kiss. "I'll be back for my shift at three o'clock."

"Stormy?" She paused to look back. "Thank you for taking care of the studio and not leaving her here."

Stormy simply smiled and nodded, then slipped out the door.

I sat in my office, wondering just how to handle this bizarre intrusion. Picking up a couple of Red Jasper stones on my desk, I ran them back and forth through my hands. Of all the Jasper stones that are common to this area, the Red Jasper was believed to encourage and enhance stamina and endurance. In fact, some people carried Red Jasper as a way of boosting their *chi*, or their life force. I liked to think of *chi* as our "juice," like an electrical current.

I had kept a Red Jasper stone on my desk and carried one since Cindy had given them to me shortly after she moved to Jasper nearly twenty years ago. It was in my purse and I was so used to having it that I nearly forgot about it.

According to some crystal experts, Red Jasper helps people face unpleasant situations and rectify unjust situations. Well, if this wasn't an unpleasant situation, I didn't know what was. I tapped the rock on my desk and took a deep breath.

Checking my watch, I stepped through the doors into the studio, clearing my throat loudly. Tamara's eyes remained shut and she continued to chant softly.

"Excuse me, Tamara?" I tried again to get her attention. She barely registered the sound, so I raised my voice.

"Tamara!"

The Goddess' eyes flew open and she looked at me wide-eyed. Her expression changed to one of shock and reproach. "Mariah, as a yoga instructor, surely you know not to interrupt someone when they are meditating?"

I nearly bit my tongue biting back the comment I wanted to say. *Remember all of those workshop payments.*

"It can't be helped this time, Tamara. I have a class coming in shortly." *Which you would have known had you waited for me with Stormy.*

Surprise flew across Tamara's face and she shook out her hands and uncrossed her legs, standing up in one fluid motion. "I wonder why that girl didn't tell me, right?"

"She did." Then I stared at the Goddess and shrugged. I could tell that discussing it with her would be a waste of both our times. As we walked to the door, I turned to Tamara. "You didn't mention needing time to 'embody' the studio when you visited the other day."

Tamara turned toward me and took one of my hands in both of hers and looked deep into my eyes. "After you left the pizzeria last night, your friends told me all about that poor woman being killed in your studio last month. I wanted to make sure that the negative energies were gone."

I pulled my hand away from hers, feeling anger well up inside, both at Tamara and whatever "friends" had ratted me out. My voice came out louder and sharper than I intended it to.

"We've had many happy experiences in the studio, before and after Patricia's death. Her passing was unbelievably sad but believe me when I say it has not impacted our energy."

I tried to smile to make up for my tone, then shoved through the doors to the lobby. Who did this Goddess person think she was coming in here and accusing my studio of bad vibes? I had thoroughly cleansed the studio, both physically and energy-wise, after the death and again after the arrest.

Fortunately, the practical part of my brain kicked into gear.

Remember the workshop payments, remember the workshop payments.

I did not want to anger the Goddess and have her pull the plug on the workshop when we'd worked so hard to make it happen.

Wheeling around to face her, I lowered my voice. "If you'd like to stay for class, you're more than welcome."

Tamara stepped away from me, her eyes narrowed and mouth pursed. She shook her head and put her hand in front of mouth as if she were pulling air out of her face. Then she threw the air to one side.

"I'm not in the right space for a class just now. I have a few things to do before I meet Deangelo later today."

With that, Tamara swept out of the lobby through the double glass doors. I watched her go and then smacked my forehead with my palm. *Stupid.* I could not afford to anger this so-called goddess if I wanted to financially survive.

The only way I had been able to bring Goddess Tamara to Jasper was by using money left to me from the student who had been killed in my class. I figured (actually, hoped and prayed) that the publicity would prove heartening for my little studio. Though the cost was considerably higher than most of my workshops, the risk seemed to be paying off.

The studio door flew open. Maya Anderson, the reporter from the local weekly, stuck her head inside. "Everything okay, Mariah? Just took a couple of snaps of the Goddess Tamara, and she did not look happy."

"Maya! You cannot put those pictures on your website!" It was all I could do to keep myself from grabbing the camera phone right out of her hands. I clasped mine together to keep from doing that. "Please, don't add to the problem."

"So everything is *not* okay?" Maya dug in her hefty shoulder bag and pulled out a notebook. "What's the scoop?"

I gave her the best stink-eye I could. "What's the scoop? Seriously?"

"Seriously. Tell me what's going on or I will have to put pictures of unhappy Tamara on my newspaper website."

I waved my hand as casually as I could. "It's nothing. Tamara just wanted to have some private time in the studio, but I have a class coming in shortly, so I couldn't let her right now. She wasn't happy about it."

"That's is?"

"That's it."

"Then why are you in such a tizzy?"

"Tizzy?" I decided honesty was the best policy. "Look, Maya, I really need for this workshop to go off well. I just can't afford any more negative publicity."

Maya gazed at me sympathetically and shrugged, shoving her notebook back into her bag. "Okay. Not much of a story anyway. But okay if I post them after the workshop?"

"Knock yourself out." I grinned at her.

Maya gave me a two-fingered salute, then ambled back out the door, no doubt going to find some other poor unsuspecting subject for her relentless camera. Don't get me wrong. As a former newspaper reporter myself, I completely understood. I just didn't like it when she pounced on me.

Blowing out a big breath of air, I hurried back into the studio to wipe down the mat Tamara had left on the floor and put out my own mat at the front of the room. I set a yoga block and a strap next to the mat to use in class. Putting a citrus scent in the diffuser, I brightened the lights so students could find their places in the studio. I looked around the room and nodded in satisfaction. I was ready. Bring on the next class.

Classes the rest of the day were uneventful, a fact I had learned to appreciate after last month's disaster. After the five o'clock Vinyasa class, Josie waited for me to lock up so we could eat at the diner on Main Street. Though I tried to convince myself to cook meals at home, it was easier and more convenient to eat out. Since my divorce, it wasn't much fun to cook just for one.

Josie tucked a backpack over her shoulder. She had changed into her sheriff's deputy uniform because she was on the night shift tonight. Before we headed to the diner, she wanted to swing by her apartment.

"I left my mascara at home. I thought I had it in my backpack."

"Really?" I looked at her askance. "That's what you need?"

She shrugged. "Everyone has their vices. Mine is having fabulous eyes!"

We laughed as we crossed the street and followed the sidewalk for a shortcut behind the Jasper Inn, the only hotel on Main Street.

We both knew I rarely even put on makeup, since I would just sweat it off during class.

"One of these days, you'll meet someone you want to wear makeup for." Josie gave me an elbow as we came around the corner. I was still laughing as Josie came to a dead stop.

"Jos-?" I started, then followed her eyes. Her mouth fell open and she stared.

Josie's little sister, Angelica, a knife in her hand, stood over a man slumped on the hotel's back steps.

Chapter 3

"Angelica, put down the knife." Josie reached behind her waist and pulled out her gun, gently slipping off the safety.

"Josie, surely you don't think you'll need that," I whispered.

"Be quiet, Mariah. I need to concentrate and do my job."

"Josie! Help! He's been hurt." Angelica waved the knife in the air as she called to her sister.

Josie took a breath and spoke firmly to her sister. "Angelica, set the knife on the ground next to the victim and put your hands in the air where I can see them."

Angelica's expression faltered. "What? Josie, I need your help. Come here."

"Angelica! Now!" Josie barked, startling her little sister.

Angelica's eyes were huge, her hands bloody. She looked at her hands as if surprised to find a knife there and quickly threw it to the ground, then reached back to pull tangled hair away from her face. She spotted the blood on her hands and slowly raised them in the air.

"Step away from the body." Josie's voice shook ever so slightly. If you didn't know how strong her voice normally was, you probably couldn't even tell. But I could.

"Josie, what are you doing?" Angelica reached her hands toward her sister.

"Hands up!" Josie barked again, then turned to flip on her shoulder radio, requesting backup and an ambulance.

She stepped closer to Angelica and kicked away the knife, then tucked her gun in its holster and leaned down over the man, whose face was turned away from us. She shook her head before turning to look hard at her sister.

"What happened?"

"I don't know, I don't know." Angelica's voice was a squeak. "I was supposed to meet Tamara upstairs and when I came up the sidewalk, I saw him lying there."

"Why did you have a knife in your hand?"

"I took it out. It seemed wrong that it was in him, so I pulled it out. Then he started bleeding more."

The man looked dead from where I was, but even I knew dead men don't bleed. Josie tucked her gun back in her belt and leaned over him again, reaching a finger to his neck.

"His pulse is faint, but I think it's there."

I scooted next to him and leaned down toward his mouth. "Oh my gosh, it's Jerry McIntyre. Jerry? Jerry, can you hear me?"

Jerry coughed, then gasped. His eyelids fluttered. "Goddess," he whispered.

"What? Jerry, I could hardly hear you." I motioned Josie down next to me so we could both hear him. "Jerry?"

As if on cue, sirens blared in the background, growing louder with every breath. Josie looked at me and shook her head. We couldn't have heard him even if he had tried to speak again.

Two sheriff's pickups screeched to a halt in the parking lot. Cindy jumped out of one car. Neil Samuelson hopped out of the other.

Josie waved them over. "I got a pulse on the second try. He might have a chance."

"Who is it?" Cindy peered around Josie.

"Jerry McIntyre from Corner Mercantile."

Cindy went to the other side of Jerry and gently lifted his face. She leapt to her feet as two paramedics bounded toward her. "Let's get him in there, STAT!"

While the paramedics worked on Jerry, Josie turned to her sister. She pulled out a small notebook. "Tell me exactly what happened."

I hovered around the steps, trying to stay out of everyone's way. They were the proverbial well-oiled machine, however, and just worked around me. Josie interviewed her sister, her face a mask. Angelica, though not quite as beautiful as her big sister, had a quiet beauty of her own, though it was hard to see it right now. Her eyes were wide, her hair was a rats' nest, and she breathed hard as deputies swabbed her hands for the blood evidence.

Glancing at my phone, I realized Josie and I were not going to make it to the diner for dinner. Cindy, either, for that matter. I texted CeCe my apologies. She was not going to be happy with us, but there was nothing to be done about it.

CeCe responded quickly as if she had been waiting to hear from me. *We heard the news. No worries. See you at breakfast.*

I frowned at my phone. CeCe normally liked her world orderly and predictable, well, as predictable as it can be when one is hyped up on her shop's caffeine. And how had they heard the news so fast? News practically travels by osmosis in small towns.

I was still frowning when Neil appeared at my side. "Mariah, are you all right?"

I nodded, clasping my arms around me in a hug, keeping my phone handy. "It's hard to believe, though. I just talked to Jerry this morning at the store. He … never mind."

"Never mind, what?"

"He seemed … sober. A lot different than last night at the pizza place."

Neil awkwardly patted my shoulder, then pulled a small notebook from his pocket. My eyes riveted to that teeny-tiny, infernal notebook.

"Oh no, not again. Not the notebook. We're doing this again?"

Neil's brow furrowed as he went into another pocket for a pen. "Did you walk into another crime scene?"

"Well, yes."

"Then we're doing it again. So, what did you see?"

Tucking my phone back in my jacket pocket, I told him how we had come around the corner to find Angelica holding the knife.

"She was standing over him with a knife?" He repeated the words, an incredulous expression on his face. "Are you sure?"

"Of course, I'm sure, and her hands were bloody, but-"

"But what?"

"She didn't look to me like she had just stabbed someone."

"Because you've seen how many people stab someone?" He raised an eyebrow as he scribbled in his infernal notebook.

I fixed a cold gaze on him. "You asked what I saw and I'm telling you."

"You're giving me commentary."

"Then go ask someone else." I huffed out a breath. "Oh, wait, you can't. Josie and I were the only ones there."

We both heavy-sighed at each other, then turned as one to look at the man on the steps. As the paramedics lifted him onto the gurney, a piece of paper fell from his hand.

"Look, Neil. He had something in his hand."

Neil was already moving toward the paper, so I scooted behind him, so close I stepped on his heels. He turned to look at me.

"Mariah, are you a law enforcement officer?"

I bit my lip and shook my head.

"Then stay out of the crime scene."

I pointed frantically at the piece of paper, which I could see was crumbled and damp. Neil pulled an evidence bag from his pocket, slipped on gloves and reached down with his pencil to pick up the paper.

He held it up so I could see it, which I thought was a gesture of conciliation until I realized the paper was a flyer for Tamara's "Find Your Goddess Within" workshop.

Neil's eyes met mine for a beat longer than necessary. I wasn't sure whether that was good or bad, so I broke my eyes away and looked toward the ground. I spied a small red stone that was partly caked in dirt. I started to reach for it and stopped myself.

"Neil." I waved him back over and pointed to the rock. "That rock doesn't look like it belongs here on the sidewalk."

Neil frowned at the rock then at me. "It's hard to say how long it's been there, Mariah."

"Perhaps your deputies missed it and it's evidence."

Neil bristled, but instead of chewing me out, he reached into a pocket and pulled out an evidence bag. He calmly reached down and picked up the stone, pausing to consider it, then dropped it into the bag. He looked me square in the eyes as he sealed the bag. "There. Happy?"

My shoulders dropped and my mouth fell open at his condescending attitude. "If it's important, you'll thank me."

"Anything else you want to tell me about the crime scene, Mariah?" Neil's voice had just a touch of irritation. I wanted to hold back and not tell him anything else, but I knew he had to know what Jerry had said. I told Neil how Jerry had mumbled "goddess."

Neil blew out a breath. "You're sure that's what he said? Did anyone else hear?"

"I'm sure, and no. Right after he said it, the paramedics arrived and it was too loud."

Neil stood deep in thought, one hand clasping the evidence bag and his notebook, the other covered his mouth. He quirked an eyebrow in my direction. "He said 'goddess.' You're sure?"

"You already asked me that. I'm sure. I wish I wasn't. He said 'goddess'."

As if on cue, the back door of the hotel opened. The Yoga Goddess stepped one foot out the door and looked quickly around as if she was seeing who was around. She stopped when she saw the crowd of people at the bottom of the steps and then jolted as Deangelo ran into her from the back.

A soft click behind me distracted me. Maya Anderson stood there, her smart phone zeroed in on Tamara and Deangelo. She saw me looking, raised her eyebrows and shrugged, then turned and walked toward Jerry's body, her camera clicking along the way.

"What's going on?" Tamara stepped further onto the porch and gasped when she saw Jerry lying on the gurney, his face covered with an oxygen mask as paramedics fought to save his life. "Who is that? What happened?"

Neil stepped smartly past the gurney and up the stairs. "It's Jerry McIntyre, Tamara. Do you know him?"

Tamara blew out a breath. "Of course," she said in a voice that sounded much different than the breathy one she had used at my studio. "We used to visit here when I was a kid, remember? We talked about it last night. I went to their store a lot."

Neil eyed her and pursed his lips, then motioned for her to move down the stairs. She paused at the gurney, an odd expression on her face, then lifted her shoulders and turned away.

"Anderson!" Neil's bark brought everyone's eyes toward him, except Maya's. She was focused on the scene around the ambulance. Without looking at Neil, she tucked her phone into her purse and pulled out a notebook, looking at him expectantly.

"No comment, Anderson. We don't know what we're dealing with yet. Go over to the sidewalk until we're done." Neil pointed toward where a small crowd of onlookers had gathered.

"People have a right to know what's going on, Detective." Maya's feet stayed where they were.

"They will, as soon as we know. Now move, before I arrest you for obstruction."

Maya reluctantly backed up to the sidewalk, keeping her eyes on the scene before her. For a small-town reporter, she sure didn't miss much.

I scooted over next to her. "How did you get here so fast?"

Maya shrugged. "I was in the neighborhood and saw the crowd. My nose always knows when news is happening."

"Do you know Jerry well?"

She shrugged. "As well as anyone, I guess. He made the crime blotter enough with his 'drunk and disorderly'."

Angelica was taken to the sheriff's station as Tamara and Deangelo were questioned inside the hotel. Josie had maintained her usual firm demeanor maintaining the crime scene, but as her sister was driven off, her face crumbled. She ducked her chin toward her chest and turned away. She looked toward me with a half-hearted wave, then turned to walk down the street to the station, her head down.

Neil pulled me back over toward the hotel steps and finished taking my statement. Then he peered at me straight in the eyes. "Mariah, you've been very helpful. Now go home. Let the Sheriff's Department handle this."

My mouth fluttered open a few times as I tried to stammer out a response that I had been quite helpful in the last investigation.

"Mariah, go home."

From Neil's tone, it sounded like an order. I took it as a suggestion, however, and headed immediately to CeCe's Coffee Shop. Maybe I could catch her before she left and we could still do dinner together and talk about Jerry's assault. It wasn't super late.

Chairs were turned upside down on the tables at the coffee shop, but I could see CeCe through the windows. I tapped at the front door. She greeted me with a surprised look on her face.

"What's up? I thought you were being grilled over at the hotel."

She stood at the door, casually blocking the entrance. I made a face. "Ha ha. We just got done so I came to see if you still wanted dinner. Glad I caught you."

"Well, um." CeCe turned to look over her shoulder. I caught a glimpse of her head barista, Paul, wiping down the counter. "I'm kind of busy."

Realization dawned and my mouth fell open. "What? You're standing me up?"

"That's not fair. You stood me up first." CeCe stood in the doorway, her hand on her hip. "So I filled in the blank. But I will see you in the morning."

She gently closed the door and locked it. With a little wave of her fingers, she turned back toward the interior of her shop.

I closed my mouth, then sighed and wondered if I had any food at home.

Chapter 4

Right after the morning Sun Salutations class, I locked the studio and sprinted to CeCe's. Eating before doing an hour of mostly Sun Salutations makes me nauseous, which means I'm typically starving by the time I finish this class. I was beginning to wish I hadn't scheduled it for two days a week.

I hadn't heard yet from Josie this morning, but she and Cindy often met us for breakfast at CeCe's. Cindy was the only one of the four of us married, so we made it a point to get together for meals when we could.

CeCe looked in my direction as the door dinged over my head. She wiped her hands on the apron around her waist and bustled over to meet me at a table. She sat down quickly.

"How are you doing? I can't believe you and Josie found Jerry. Did you hear the latest?"

"I'm fine. What's the latest?"

"He didn't make it."

I closed my eyes and nodded. He had seemed so close to death last night that I could feel it.

All of the small business owners on Main Street knew each other, including Sandy and Jerry. We all knew Jerry hadn't been running the Corner Mercantile for the past few years, perhaps longer. Sandy had been holding down that particular family fort. I'd tried to get Sandy to take a break and come practice yoga with us, but she had not yet taken me up on my offer of a free class or two, even when bags hung under her eyes and large creases framed her face, her dish-water blond hair hanging behind in a limp pony tail.

"I'll try," she usually told me with a weary smile. "It's tough to get away from this place sometimes."

I leaned back, letting my head relax on the booth. "I feel so bad for him and for Sandy. How did she take the news?"

CeCe unconsciously wiped at the table with a cloth and shrugged, then looked up as Josie slid into the booth across from me.

"She took it as well as can be expected." Josie answered my question as she sipped her coffee – straight up black – out of a to-go cup.

"Why are you wearing your uniform? I thought you were on night patrol."

"*Your* sister put me on the front desk until the case against *my* sister is closed."

My mouth made a little "o" as CeCe and I exchanged glances.

Josie just shook her head, spinning the cup with her fingers. "It's okay. I get it. I mean, I don't get it, but I get it. Ya know?"

"Did you get that?" I turned to CeCe.

"I got it."

Josie stared at us. Her expression said she was not amused.

"It's just like—"

"Don't even say it, Mariah." Josie's face turned sour as she held up a hand. "It is not just like when you were accused of murder and Cindy couldn't help solve it. At least she got to keep doing her job. I'm stuck on desk duty."

She picked up her coffee fiercely, spilling some over the edge. CeCe leaned forward to wipe it up but stopped when she saw Josie's expression. She backed up. "I'm just going to get you both some pastries. Sit tight."

She jumped up and scooted away, leaving me to handle Josie in a way that didn't involve sweets.

"To be fair, Cindy is an elected official, so she got to keep her job." Josie turned her stone-faced gaze to me, so I sped things up. "What can I do to help?"

Josie shrugged and shook her head.

"Josie, you have been my friend since I moved here. You're always there for me. You even come to yoga class when I know you don't really like it all that much."

A smile played at Josie's mouth. Then she turned serious again as she looked at me across the table, her dark eyes seeming even darker than usual.

"I feel so helpless, Mariah. Neil has both Angelica and Deangelo in his sights and I don't know how to stop him."

I remembered that feeling well. "Josie, remember *satya*. We talked about it in class the other day."

She frowned. "*Satya*. Like truthfulness?"

"Something like that. *Satya* is being able to see the truth in situations without judgment, just seeing things as they really are." I peered at her more closely. "Keep an open mind and eventually, truth will out. I really believe that."

"That seems easier to do than *ahimsa* right now."

"Why do you say that?" I was a little afraid of what her answer might be. *Ahimsa*, another of yoga's guiding principles, referred to nonviolence.

"Because when I find out who actually killed Jerry, it might be hard for me to stay non-violent."

I laughed awkwardly, hoping she was making a joke, but Josie didn't laugh with me. I looked around the table for my usual mocha, then realized I had forgotten to order it in my rush to talk with CeCe. I looked toward the counter and mimed drinking coffee to CeCe. She nodded and reached for a coffee mug. I turned back to Josie, relieved that my coffee was on the way.

"Will you help me?" Josie sat a little bit straighter and leaned across the table. "I cannot even believe I'm saying this, but seriously.

You and CeCe were good at talking to all those people when Neil was focused on you. Maybe you can help me find a way to prove Angelica is innocent?"

I reached across the table and covered Josie's hand with mine. "Of course, we'll do anything we can to help."

"We will?" CeCe stood by the table with a small plate with both plain and chocolate-filled croissants and a mocha for me.

"Double shot? Extra chocolate?"

CeCe brushed away my questions, her eyes on Josie's. Worry lines creased her face as she sat down, sliding the croissants to the middle and the mocha in front of me. I sipped the mocha, relieved to taste the strong extra shot of coffee and the extra chocolate.

"Weren't you the one who said we should let qualified law-enforcement officers handle the investigation?" CeCe did not sound happy. " 'Don't get involved,' you told us. 'Stay out of Neil's way,' you told us. Now you want us to help you?"

CeCe crossed her arms and stared across the table.

Josie dropped her eyes toward her cup. "Well, to be honest, I was really only asking Mariah."

She reached for a croissant, but CeCe jerked the plate away.

"You don't think I can help?"

Josie started laughing and I joined in.

"She's just messing with you." I gently took the plate from CeCe and pushed it toward Josie, who quickly pulled off part of the croissant, then shoved it into her mouth before CeCe could snatch it back.

"Of course, we'll help, Josie." I nibbled on my own piece of croissant as I made eye contact with CeCe. She nodded subtly, then uncrossed her arms and stared at the spot of spilled coffee on the table.

"It's killing you, isn't it?" Josie spoke between bites.

CeCe nodded.

"Okay, you can clean it up."

Breathing a heavy sigh of relief, CeCe reached over and wiped the table as Josie lifted her cup so she could swipe underneath. The coffee house owner's fits of neatness were fodder for jokes and pranks, but in the end, we did try to help her keep her business clean.

I had been thinking as CeCe swiped at the table. "This is a good idea. We can totally help clear Angelica. We figured out who killed Patricia before the cops did."

"Sheriff's deputies." Josie quickly corrected me.

"Whatever."

"You also almost got yourself killed."

I closed my mouth, biting back a retort and sitting back in my seat.

"Yeah, that's actually true." I turned to CeCe. "We just need to figure out who did it, then get out of the way and let the cops handle it."

"So we don't die."

"Yes, so we don't die."

"Sounds like a good plan." CeCe sat back, unconsciously folding the cloth into fourths and setting it on the table in front of her as Josie and I chewed and sipped in silence.

"What is the evidence against Angelica, besides that she was standing over the body with the murder weapon?" I figured we might as well start gathering the details. "Which is a problem, by the way. Also, she's really strong. I've seen her in class."

Josie licked her fingers, then used them to tick off the reasons.

"One, she had means, obviously – she was holding the knife that killed Jerry when we found her." She ticked off another finger. "Two, she had opportunity on the back steps of the hotel where she was going to meet Tamara and, three, they said she has motive because she was trying to protect Tamara. Plus, she has a fairly lengthy rap sheet from her druggie days."

"Angelica does drugs?" I sat up straighter and stared at Josie. "I don't see that at all."

Josie smiled and nodded. "*Did* drugs. She's been clean for three years. Yoga actually helped her a lot, that and twelve-step programs."

I wasn't surprised that yoga had helped her get clean and sober. A teacher of mine told me that once a student begins practicing yoga, she can change other areas of her life as well.

"I remember hearing about her." CeCe pulled off a piece of croissant. "Seems like she was in the Jasper crime blotter every other week."

"For what?" This did not sound at all like the Angelica I had met.

"Petty crime, mostly." Josie played with the plate holding the croissants and suddenly wouldn't make eye contact. "But she did have one assault charge toward the end. She took on some guy in a bar over in Auburn. With a knife."

Chapter 5

I stared at Josie. "You might have led with that, or at least mentioned it sooner."

This new information potentially changed things. If Neil felt Angelica had a history of stabbing people, of course he would keep her in jail. I probably would, too.

Josie played with her cup, emotions angling for room on her face. "Look, one of the reasons the charge was dropped was that she got clean as part of the deal. Plus, it's not like it's a pattern. It happened one time."

The bell dinged at the front of the coffee shop and, as we nearly always did, our heads swiveled toward the door to see who had arrived. Jennifer Parks stepped in, her face tilted downward.

CeCe glanced at the empty take-out counter and jumped up to greet her and take her order. She opened her eyes wide and kept nodding toward Jennifer, like she was trying to send us a coded message. My brow furrowed as I peered at her, then shrugged.

"Do you see CeCe?"

"I don't know what she wants us to do," Josie responded as she took another sip from her cup but kept looking toward the counter.

Jennifer turned around as she waited for her order and saw us watching. Her eyes, rimmed with red, seemed lost as her face puckered.

I waved her over. She shook her head, so I slipped out of the booth.

"Jennifer, are you okay?"

She shook her head again and tears welled up in her eyes. "I just heard about Jerry. He was a friend, ya know?"

I patted her shoulder. "I'm so sorry. Were you close?"

She nodded. "He was a great guy, so generous. Who would do such a thing?" Then Jennifer realized Josie was sitting in the booth and she strode over to her.

"Your sister. Did you sister do this? Did she kill Jerry?"

Josie sat up straight, her dark eyes flashing. She struggled to maintain her calm, but I could tell it was a battle. She slipped out of the booth so she stood taller than Jennifer and took a deep breath. "Jennifer, this isn't the time or place."

"Did she?" Jennifer's voice grew louder. "She always thought she could do whatever she wanted here and look what happened. I'm glad she's in jail for what she did to him."

"Jennifer, it's time for you to leave."

She wiped at her face, leaving streaks from the tears and snot on her cheeks. CeCe reached around her and handed her two paper coffee cups in a carrier along with a pastry bag. Jennifer took it without acknowledging CeCe, her eyes on Josie. Her face seemed to crumple in on itself before she turned and lurched toward the door. Maya Anderson appeared outside and put an arm around her friend as they walked away.

The three of us stood in awkward silence, then slipped back into the booth.

"That was interesting." Josie sipped her coffee, holding the mug with both hands.

"That's an understatement." I picked up my mocha. "We're going to need to talk with Jennifer Parks some more. Maya Anderson, too."

"Why Maya?" CeCe turned a puzzled face toward me.

"Last night, she talked about Jerry as if he was already dead. How would she have known that?"

We sat in silence for a few moments. I needed to change the subject.

"So, CeCe, how was your date last night?" I tried to act casual.

CeCe smiled and refolded the cloth in front of her.

"Date? What date? You were supposed to have dinner with us." Josie sat up straighter and peered at CeCe, who shrugged.

"You stood me up."

"Because of a *murder*."

CeCe smiled, her eyes wide. "I'm not ready to talk about it – or him – yet."

"You've been saying that for over a month now." Josie and I reached for the last of the chocolate croissant at the same time. I backed away, figuring she needed the sugar more than I did today.

"Soon." CeCe smiled, then slipped back out of the seat and skipped down the aisle back to the coffee counter.

"This Paul thing might be more serious than she is letting on." Josie wiped her fingers on her napkin as she watched CeCe step behind the counter and greet a customer. "I haven't seen her this happy in a long time."

CeCe's divorce was brutal – and legendary – in Jasper. It happened before I moved here to be closer to Cindy, but I still heard most of the details about her ex-husband. If what I'd heard was accurate, most men in town were afraid to get on CeCe's bad side.

I followed her eyes toward CeCe, leaning my chin on my hand.

"Don't you have a class or something?" Josie interrupted my thoughts.

"Oh, crumb!" I jumped up, paused to swig the rest of my mocha, and raced out the door.

Chapter 6

The morning fairly flew. By the time the noon class rolled around, I had marked off most of my lengthy to-do list. The front door opened with regularity by about a quarter to twelve, as students popped in for a mid-day yoga break. The class was typically filled with students who wanted to sweat along with their stretches.

I put a citrus scent in the diffuser to energize the air and began to greet students. About ten minutes before class was to start, as I was taking a credit card payment in the office, the lobby and studio area went silent. Puzzled, I poked my head through the office door to see what had changed the atmosphere.

Goddess Tamara stood tentatively in the lobby. She smiled as I walked toward her, then enveloped me in a hug.

"Welcome back to The Yoga Mat, Tamara. Did you want to look around a little more?" My voice was calm, but on the inside all I could think was *please, please, please don't stay for class*. I wasn't sure my nerves were up to teaching a class with the Goddess Tamara in attendance.

"Actually, Mariah, I hoped to attend your class today." *Dang it.* "With all that's going on at the hotel, I just needed to get out and find a good space. You don't mind, right?" She looked at me tentatively.

"No, of course, I don't. You are more than welcome here." Yes, of course, I lied. No way was I going to admit she made me nervous. A celebrity yogi in my class? No problem.

I showed her where to store her things, and she insisted on paying the drop-in fee, which made me think a little more highly of her. She didn't think she was so important she didn't have to pay the fees. Then she slipped off her sandals and padded toward the back row of the class. She quietly set down her mat and settled into place, crossing her legs in Easy Pose and closing her eyes.

My students watched her every move, even those who pretended to be busy with their own mats while she was setting out hers.

I shrugged. Okay, so the Goddess just wanted to do yoga. Who knew? After talking with Josie about *satya* at the coffee shop, I had decided to use that as a theme for classes that day. I had also planned to feature a few more Goddess poses, but that seemed awkward with the actual "goddess" in the class. I didn't want to call any more attention to her than necessary or have my students feel she was critiquing their Goddess pose.

Goddess pose can be difficult for many. Standing with legs wide on the mat, toes pointed outward at an angle, we sit straight down just before our knees want to wobble inward. This is where many go wrong as they try to keep their knees bent without splaying them outward.

I switched gears and mentally substituted Triangle and Wide-legged Forward Fold poses in place of Goddess.

As my students got centered with their eyes closed, I started off the class with the Kali mudra, instructing students to bring their arms straight out in front of them, fingers clasped with the left thumb over the right and the pointer fingers the only fingers not clasped. The Kali Mudra is generally believed to encourage a positive flow while at the same time removing any blockages.

"During class today, perhaps we can tap into the yogic principle of *satya*. Remember that *satya* calls for us to stay open to the truth, encouraging us to see things as they are instead of as we might wish them to be."

Tamara's eyes popped wide open and locked with mine, startling both of us. I gently smiled as I continued to scan the room for anyone showing signs of discomfort. Through my peripheral vision, I noticed Tamara close her eyes again and take deep breaths, and I wondered why truthfulness caused her such distress.

Once the students had begun class, they seemed to forget Tamara was there. She followed my cues, never substituting poses the way some visiting yoga teachers did. I appreciated the respect she showed to my class and to me. My opinion of her notched up quite a bit.

When class was over, Tamara quietly talked with a few of the students, although she refused to give autographs or take selfies with them.

"I'm here in my private time as a student just like you are," she told them as she gently touched their shoulders or arms before she moved on to the next person.

I ran interference as best I could, but rabid yoga fans are insistent. After finally shooing them all out the door, I turned to Tamara with a smile.

"Thank you for class today," she said as she slipped on her sandals. "I was wondering if I might come by some time before the workshop to have some alone time in the studio, just to adjust to the energy and settle into the space."

The hairs stood up on the back of my neck and I scrunched my shoulders to rid myself of the sensation. I bit my lip as I considered her request.

"I'm not sure how comfortable I am with that, Tamara." I was hesitant to explain. "We had some trouble some time ago with unwanted visitors, and I'm still a little protective of my studio right now. Let me think about it and I'll get back to you."

She looked at me in surprise, then shrugged. "Whatever works best for you, Mariah. I understand." She smiled again and floated out of the studio with a wave.

I stood at the doorway of the studio and looked around, although I knew every inch as well as my own hand. Why was she so insistent on having time alone in my studio? And why was I so hesitant to let her have some time here?

The second question was easier to answer. Just a month ago, someone had hidden a bottle of arsenic in the closet of my studio while trying to frame me for murder. Honestly, that would make anyone protective of their space. I already checked and double-checked the supply cabinet daily now, making sure nothing toxic was there. Stormy watched me do it, too. She never said anything, though. Stormy understood.

On the other hand, maybe I was just being unreasonable. It's been known to happen.

Chapter 7

CeCe and I were already at the diner, me sipping iced tea and CeCe a glass of white wine when Josie bolted through the door. She threw her bag into a chair and flung herself into the booth opposite us, her face one big scowl.

Instinctively and in unison, CeCe and I leaned away from her. Josie's shoulders drooped and she slumped in her seat.

I touched the space between my eyes. "You're going to get frown lines if you keep doing that."

"Shut up." She glared at me. I tried not to laugh. Really.

Our usual waitress plopped a large soda in front of Josie, which forced her eyes off of me and toward her aproned savior.

"Thank you, Bev. You are an angel and that is the nicest thing anyone has done for me today."

Bev guffawed. "Sounds like you've had a rough day."

Josie shook her head in response. She pointed to the television over the small bar area, where a boxing match appeared to be underway. One boxer had just been pummeled by the other. All three of us stared at it, mesmerized.

"I feel a little bit like that guy." Josie pointed to the guy on the television who was now on his knees. "Have I mentioned how much I hate desk duty? I even got a paper cut." She held a hand, her pinky swathed in a Band-aid.

"You poor baby."

"I'm so sorry you had to experience that."

CeCe and I used our sweetest fake voices. Josie made faces at us.

"At least you didn't bleed to death. You girls ready to order?" Bev whipped out her pad and we placed our orders.

We didn't have strict "usuals," but we tended to cycle through some favorites. I typically opted for a salad or Bev's homemade veggie burger, but tonight, I needed comfort food. Grilled cheese with a cup of tomato soup.

Josie's eyes went up at my order, but when she ordered meatloaf, I just laughed. Guess we all needed some comfort food tonight.

"Okay, Josie," CeCe got right down to business. "What did you learn about the case today?"

Josie sat back, her eyes distant.

"Relax your shoulders," I whispered gently. She smiled as her shoulders visibly relaxed.

It wasn't that I was some hot-shot yogi. I just did it myself: Whenever I got upset about something, my shoulders tightened so much I could practically rest my ear lobes on them.

Releasing my shoulders allowed me to focus on what was at hand rather than hold on to what was troubling me. Kind of like *satya*, I reflected, then turned my attention back to Josie.

"Angelica is still in the jail cell, although she might be released to my mom tomorrow, according to Neil," she paused here and made another face, which is typically something more that I would do, not Josie. Apparently, she was picking up my bad habits.

"I can see why Neil still has her in jail." CeCe shrugged. "It doesn't look good."

Josie leaned across the table, putting her hands down and leaning into them. "People. Change, CeCe. Angelica is not the same person she was when she was doing drugs. She has completely turned around her life. She's taking classes and planning to become a paramedic."

CeCe bit her lip as she eyed Josie. "I'm sorry. I didn't mean—"

Josie waved away her apology, but her voice sounded small. "It's okay. It doesn't look good."

"Why hasn't he let her out on bail? I mean, she's your sister." That question had been bothering me all day. "Neil knows you would make sure Angelica stays put."

"That's the problem. Neil said he knew I would, but he couldn't treat me any differently than he treated someone he didn't know as well. Seriously, he has been to my mom's house. My mother has cooked dinner for him. She made her special tamales recipe. He knows us!"

"Your mom made tamales for him? She hasn't made tamales for me."

"Not the point, Mariah."

I was still trying to decide if my feelings should be hurt when CeCe made the rolling motions with her hands to "move things along."

"Right. Moving on." I pulled a small notebook out of my bag. "Let's talk suspects."

Josie and CeCe looked at me wearily. "Do we have to?"

I looked up to see Bev striding our way with a tray of food and shoved the notebook to the side. "Naw, we can wait until after we eat."

Dinner was quieter than usual. I enjoyed my decadent and greasy grilled cheese, figuring it was harder to put my foot in my mouth if my mouth was filled with something, even greasy grilled cheese.

Josie and I both swiped potato chips from CeCe's plate. She always got chips or French fries but rarely ate them all, so we considered it "friendly food" and helped ourselves. The only time she swatted our hands away was if she got the garlic fries. Since she'd been dating Paul the barista, however, I noticed she ordered garlic fries less often.

As soon as we were finished, CeCe and I pushed our plates aside and I set the notebook in front of me. I looked at my friends expectantly.

"First, I think we need to know why Neil thinks Angelica would kill for Tamara."

CeCe gingerly wiped her hands on a napkin, glancing sideways up at Josie.

Josie played with the leftover food on her plate. "Not just Angelica. Neil is also looking at Deangelo."

Chapter 8

"Neil thinks your little sister, your little brother or both killed Jerry McIntyre?" I stared at Josie incredulously.

She pursed her lips and nodded. "Yep. He's got a pretty high opinion of the Vazquez clan right now."

"Interesting that they both have 'angel' in their names," CeCe mused, her hands playing with the stem of her wine glass, with the wine mostly gone by now.

"They were all pretty much angels after me." Josie chuckled. "I was the one that was hell on wheels."

My mouth fell open. "You? You're the most straight-laced, law-abiding person I know."

"Now I am." She wiggled her eyebrows at me.

I tapped the pen on the notepad to bring us back to the business at hand.

"Why would Neil think both of them would kill to protect Tamara? That seems like a stretch to me. I've worked for lots of people and not one of them would I be willing to kill for, not to mention men I've dated. I wouldn't even kill for my husband."

Josie and CeCe's eyebrows shot up.

"Not that he ever asked me to. Of course, he didn't."

Josie turned and stretched her legs out in the booth. "Deangelo and Tamara have been dating for a few months now. Mostly, I think she's just leading him on, but he's in it to win it."

"And Angelica works for Tamara. What does she do for her?" CeCe's forehead wrinkled as she tried to remember what she'd heard.

"She handles her social media and some other promotional stuff. It's a part-time job while she's in school. Angel interned at the same hospital where Tamara taught yoga and she became one of her 'followers'." Josie made air quotes around "followers." "Then she got hired."

I recalled Tamara's reaction to *satya* and wondered. "But why would Angelica and Deangelo think Tamara would need protecting?"

Josie went quiet. CeCe kept spinning the wine glass.

"Ladies?" I looked back and forth between the two. "Is there something in particular you'd like to share with me?"

They looked at each other and shrugged.

"It's really just gossip," CeCe said.

"Really old gossip," Josie added, leaning forward and lowering her voice. "Before she was the 'goddess,' Tamara and her family visited here in the summers, like she mentioned the other night. Then when Tamara was about fourteen--"

"About fourteen, fifteen years ago." CeCe added to the story.

Josie nodded, then continued. "Her family left abruptly right in the middle of the summer. They packed up and were gone overnight."

"Did they say why?"

Josie shook her head. "It was very hush-hush, but-- ."

"What I heard was that Jerry had assaulted Tamara at the store," CeCe finished for Josie.

My heart sank. How awful for a teen-age girl to experience such brutality.

"Her family never came back here, but rumor has it that Jerry and Sandy paid them a quarter million dollars to make the whole thing go away."

We all sat back, digesting the information as well as dinner.

"This is the first time Tamara has been back?" I looked from Josie to CeCe, who, even though she had only been here five years longer than I had, seemed particularly plugged in to this story.

They both nodded. I continued with my train of thought.

"If Tamara was fourteen when this allegedly happened, wouldn't that have been the same summer she was dating Deangelo?"

"I think 'dating' is a stretch. They were fourteen years old." If the expression on Josie's face revealed her feelings, she clearly didn't think much of the "summer romance" story.

I turned toward her, surprised at her reaction. "Josie, you have five little brothers and sisters. You couldn't possibly keep up with all of them at once. Besides, you're five or six years older than Deangelo. Weren't you away at college when this was going on?"

Josie shook her head, then paused. "Not in the summer. Oh, wait. That must have been the summer I worked for the Forest Service. I was out in the field for days at a time."

Josie breathed in relief. As the eldest sibling in her family, she had helped to raise the others. I could tell it bothered her that she hadn't remembered this important relationship for her kid brother.

"Whatever it was, did Deangelo know about it? Would she have told him?" I wasn't sure if it was a rhetorical question or I really expected someone to answer it.

Josie shrugged. "He never mentioned it to me."

"Neil thinks Angelica or Deangelo killed Jerry out of revenge for Tamara for something that happened fifteen years ago?"

They nodded again.

That seemed unlikely. I did some neck rolls to relax, my attention drawn back to the television. Bev had turned down the sound, but I could still see the kicks and punches. I flinched when one boxer hit the other hard in the jaw. The other guy dropped to the mat.

I shuddered. "How can people do such violence to each other?"

Josie's face puckered. "Mariah, we're here discussing a murder, so this fake fighting on TV is not even in the same category."

"You really think it's fake? I'm not sure. He looked like he really got hurt there. Oh!" I flinched again, then dragged my attention away to find Josie and CeCe staring at me. "It's hard to look away."

"Focus, Mariah."

I took a breath and looked at the nearly empty pad of paper in front of me. My reporter training had kicked in as we discussed the evidence. I took a deep breath. "Josie, I know you don't want to hear this, but it has to be said. It has to be in the open."

As if she knew what I was about to say, Josie crossed her arms and stared boldly at me. "Then say it."

I looked at CeCe for help. Her eyes were big.

"You haven't been around either Angelica or Deangelo for several years. They were really kids when you knew them well. What if they've changed in L.A.?"

The silence was palpable. Josie slowly shook her head and began to uncross her arms. "We were raised in the same house. I just can't see it. They are not perfect people, but they're not killers." She cracked a small smile. "Besides, they know if they did it, my mom would kill them."

We all laughed in relief, then I looked at each of them in turn. "If it's not them, who is it?"

Chapter 9

I took the initiative and wrote down Sandy in the column on my paper under the word "suspects." Then I looked back up at my friends. "We have to write down the spouse. That's common practice."

Josie burst into laughter. If it hadn't been aimed toward me, I would have been happy to see her smile. "Mariah, don't you think Neil already thought of that? He questioned her extensively right after Jerry died."

"And?"

"And she has an alibi for the time of the murder. She was stocking shelves at the store. Her part-time cashier – what's his name, Sammy? – was working the front counter and said she was there the whole time."

I made a face and drew a line through her name.

CeCe tapped the notebook in front of me. "Put Tamara on the list."

I jotted her name beneath Sandy's. "It does seem suspicious that Jerry was killed just when Tamara came to town for the first time in years."

"Right. And she seems so fake." Josie pointed at the list with her straw. "There's a lot we don't know about her. Where has she been for the past fifteen years? Why did she come back now?"

"Um, Josie? She came back because I invited her to do a workshop at The Yoga Mat."

Josie's face fell. "Right. I knew that. I just got carried away."

Josie wanted the murderer to be someone we didn't know well. Me, too. It's hard to believe someone you know would kill another person.

"Okay, who else?"

We stared around the table at each other, then looked at the ceiling and the floor.

"This might sound strange, but what about Lou Alveretti?" My gaze bounced between CeCe and Josie.

"Lou who owns Luigi's Pizzeria?" CeCe pulled away and looked at me, her expression one of comical disbelief.

I told them about the looks that had passed between Sandy and Lou the other night at the pizzeria. "It just seemed like something else was going on with them."

Josie and CeCe sat quickly, both nodding their heads as they mulled over this new information.

"Maybe."

"I could see it."

"I've always felt sorry for Sandy, having to make a go of the store with little to no help from Jerry." CeCe spoke from experience, having had to take over the coffee shop after her ex-husband bailed on her.

"She could have divorced him," I protested. I hated it when people verbally make victims of others. "She would've had a good case."

Josie vigorously shook her head. "Mariah, people in relationships with addicts and alcoholics often get really confused and stay longer than they might otherwise."

"Okay, who else?"

I paused and tapped my chin with the pencil. "Here's another strange one. What about Jennifer Parks?"

CeCe laughed out loud. "The Safety Blanket lady? Why would she kill Jerry McIntyre?"

I shrugged, then told them what I had seen at the Corner Mercantile the morning Jerry died. When I finished, CeCe tapped the notebook again.

"Write her down. After the way she acted today in the shop, maybe I could see it."

As I dutifully added Jennifer's name to the list, Josie sat back in the booth, a puzzled expression on her face. "Mariah, how is it that you notice all of these things? First, Lou and Sandy and now Jennifer and Jerry? I've lived here all my life, I'm a deputy, and I totally missed all that."

I sat back and shrugged. "Probably just my reporter experience. My newspaper friends and I used to quiz each other to see what we noticed. If we walked into a restaurant, they might ask me 'how many people were sitting at the bar?', that kind of thing. I guess I still just notice stuff."

"Thank goodness. I figured it had to do with all the yoga and I was going to have to do more of it." She grinned at me. "And we both know that wouldn't end well."

Just then the bell dinged over the front door. I glanced up to see Sheriff's Detective Neil Samuelson walk through. He gave me a nod, then headed straight to the counter to order food to go.

As he waited, he wandered over to our table, grabbing a chair from nearby, spinning it around and sitting backward on it next to us.

He looked at me fondly. I tried not to sparkle back.

"What are we chatting about tonight, ladies?"

Oops. There was an awkward moment as we looked at each other, then shrugged.

"Not much," CeCe finally said. "Girl stuff."

Neil looked at each of us in turn, finally landing on me. "You wouldn't be talking about the Jerry McIntyre murder, would you?"

I averted my eyes, then sat up a little straighter and turned back to him. "Of course, we're talking about Jerry's murder. It's the biggest thing that's happened in town since, well, since I was accused of killing a student."

I looked at him pointedly.

Neil's mouth fell open and he leaned away from me. "You have seriously got to give me a break on that. I was just doing my job."

"I was just doing my job." Yes, I mocked him. Sometimes, I just can't help myself.

"Order up!" Bev barked from behind the counter.

Neil stood up, and roughly shoved the chair back under the neighboring table. He strode to the counter and took his bag of food from Bev. Pausing at our table, he looked me in the eye. "Just remember, Mariah, you almost got yourself killed playing detective last time. Leave the investigation to the Sheriff's Department."

He turned and strode from the diner.

We sat silently, then started to giggle.

"We're going to talk to Lou Alveretti tomorrow, right?" CeCe looked at me as she started gathering her things.

"Definitely."

Chapter 10

CeCe pulled my arm before I could open the door. "Are you sure we need to do this?" she hissed as she looked down the street. I followed her gaze.

"Who are you looking for?"

"No one, you dope." She swatted me on the arm. "I just don't think this is a good idea."

My shoulders dropped and I crossed my arms over my chest. "We promised Josie we'd help Angelica and find some more suspects." Now it was my turn to look around. "Clearly Lou is a suspect."

She rolled her eyes. "I think you might have been reading more into a situation than what was there."

I stopped with one hand on the door and one on my hip. "We have to talk to him now before he gets busy with the lunch crowd." I took a whiff of the air. "Besides, I'm hungry and pizza sounds good."

I bolted through the door before CeCe could stop me. It's not that I disagreed with her. I just wanted to follow through on my promise to Josie. Sometimes, throwing myself bodily into a room was the best way to make the rest of me follow.

I stopped so suddenly that CeCe slammed into my back, her elbow nearly knocking the wind out of me.

Lou stood just outside the kitchen door, his back to us, his voice raised to a yell at someone inside.

"When I tell you to do something, I expect you to follow my directions – exactly as I give them. Don't improvise. Don't change anything. It's the way it is for a reason. You have already destroyed hundreds of dollars' worth of ingredients doing things your own way. This is your last chance, and then you're out on your ear, I don't care who your parents are."

He threw down a dish towel on the counter and spun toward us so suddenly I jerked back toward CeCe. I don't know about CeCe, but my mouth fell open in disbelief. In all the times I had been in the restaurant, I had never seen this side of Lou.

Lou jerked to a halt, his face red from exertion. "Um, welcome, ladies." He glanced back to the kitchen, then moved toward us, motioning us into the just-opened restaurant. No other customers were inside yet. He motioned to a table. "Come in and have a seat."

"Let's go, let's go, let's go," CeCe hissed in my ear.

"We can't." I tried to talk out of the side of my mouth to her, but it apparently didn't work because Lou looked at us with a puzzled expression on his face, then he went to fetch menus and glasses.

CeCe and I sat gingerly in our chairs with the red plastic covers and studied Lou. He looked to be pushing fifty but still had a full head of hair and only a slight paunch at his stomach. Frankly, he seemed in surprisingly good shape for someone who worked – and, I assumed, ate – pizza and pasta every day.

Lou set down menus and glasses at our table. He waved a hand toward the kitchen. "Sorry you had to see that. New kitchen help. Thinks his mom's pizza recipes are better than mine and my dad's." He smiled sheepishly as he quickly filled the glasses with ice water.

I picked up a menu and passed another to CeCe. "Is it hard to get decent help these days?"

Lou shrugged. "It ebbs and flows. Right now, it's kind of a down time for hiring. It will pick up again."

Lou walked back toward the kitchen.

"What are you doing?" CeCe held her menu in front of us and whispered to me behind it.

I peeked over the menu to make sure no one was listening, then I whispered back. "I'm trying to make small talk and maybe bond with him as small-business owners, you know, lull him into a false sense of security before we pounce."

CeCe rolled her eyes, then put them back on the menu, still held up in front of our faces.

"This is ridiculous," she said, a little too loudly. "And, by the way, cliché."

"Not the menu, I hope." Lou's voice came from just the other side of the wall we had made with our menus.

CeCe blushed and peeked over the top, lowering hers down and guiding mine to the table as well. "No, no, not at all. My partner in crime here sometimes has ridiculous ideas about things."

Lou turned toward me and smiled. "I've heard great things about Mariah's ideas from customers who go to her classes."

I turned toward CeCe and preened, then remembered why we were there.

"So, Lou," I set down my menu and—

"Do you serve fake chicken here? Mariah doesn't eat meat."

Lou leaned back as CeCe interrupted me. I turned and glared at her.

"You mean like soy products?" He shook his head. "I don't carry them because most are heavily processed and not in huge demand."

"See, I told you." CeCe looked at me and smiled triumphantly. "You really should stick to more whole foods, Mariah."

Lou looked back and forth between us. "Perhaps I'll come back in a minute to take your order." He stepped quickly away, then stopped at the door to the kitchen to throw us a puzzled glance.

CeCe and I glared at each other.

"What are you doing?" I hissed at her. "I was going to ask him about his alibi."

"Before we've ordered? Do you *want* him to spit on our pizza?"

"Shhh, he's right there."

We glanced toward the kitchen, where Lou was working, then lifted our menus up in front of our faces again.

"He is not going to spit on our pizza."

"You don't know that."

"Right now, *I* would spit on your pizza. I cannot believe we are having this conversation."

"Because you're about to get us in big trouble," CeCe hissed. "We can't just go around accusing fellow Main Street business owners of murder. There's got to be some kind of professional code that bars that."

"There's no code, CeCe." I breathed deeply, then set down the menu and looked squarely at CeCe. "Let's compromise. We will order and pay for our pizzas, and I get to ask as many questions as I want while we wait just so long as I don't accuse him of murder. That way, Lou will be here with us and we will know he is not in the kitchen spitting on our pizza."

CeCe made a face that looked like she'd just swallowed a centipede. "How is that a compromise?"

My mouth opened as I started to speak, then I quickly closed it. "Don't look now, but look who just floated in."

CeCe's face puckered like she'd like to spit the centipede at me. "How can I look if I'm not supposed to look?"

Too late. Deangelo and Tamara saw us and waved, then walked toward us.

"Mind if we join you?"

We looked at each other and shrugged.

Tamara picked up on our tentativeness. "Unless you're having a girl-talk lunch. Then we can eat over there."

"Yes, that's it."

"No, it's fine. Sit down."

CeCe and I spoke at the same time. She looked at me with a little smile on her face. I sighed in defeat and waved my hand across from us.

"Please, join us."

They sat down and started discussing the pizza.

"I'm surprised you two are here today, since you just had pizza the other night." The words were out of my mouth before I really thought about them.

Tamara looked at me. "You can't have too much pizza, right? Besides, you were there with us when we had pizza the other night. If it's not too much for you, it must be okay then, right?"

Just because she added "right?" to the ends of her sentences did not mean I was going to agree with her.

I turned my attention to Deangelo, who sat down with an unhappy thud.

"Not a pizza fan, Deangelo?"

He flashed me a weak smile, then threw a glare toward Tamara, who sat with her hands clasped on the table, looking toward the kitchen.

"Let's just say it's not my first choice today. Someone insisted."

"Welcome back to Luigi's Pizza, Goddess." Lou was suddenly there, with a tray with glasses of ice water for Deangelo and Tamara. I was glad for the intrusion because Deangelo's words and, more importantly, his tone had left me momentarily speechless.

CeCe raised her hand. "Could we get some water, too, please?"

Lou nodded shortly without looking at her. "What can I get for you, Tamara?"

Deangelo's eyes flickered from the menu at Tamara, then quickly down again.

"You're Luigi, right?" Tamara leaned her head on her hand with her elbow on the table as she looked up at Lou.

Lou laughed, his cheeks flushing. "I am the owner of Luigi's, as I mentioned the other night. My dad was Luigi, but I go by Lou. Just plain ole Lou."

Tamara giggled. "Of course, just plain ole Lou. I was just teasing." She glanced down at the menu, then gazed back at Lou. "What would you recommend?"

"For you, the specialty vegetarian, without the onions."

Tamara brought her hand to her heart. "You remembered. That's so sweet. We'll have that." She tried to hand the menu back to Lou, but Deangelo held on to it.

"Actually," he started. "we'll have half vegetarian, half sausage and pepperoni."

Without looking at Tamara, he closed the menu and handed it to Lou. "And two sparkling waters, please."

Lou looked at Tamara as if to make sure the order was okay with her, but her gaze was fixed on Deangelo. Lou turned toward the kitchen.

CeCe held up her hands. "Thank you for taking our order as well," she muttered.

I leaned toward her. "To be fair, we were being difficult."

Tamara hissed at Deangelo. "You know I don't like meat near my food."

Deangelo sipped from his water glass without looking at her. "I'm sure it won't kill you, just this once."

We sat in awkward silence, broken only when Lou dropped off the sparkling waters. Tamara mouthed "thank you" to him as she accepted hers, as if she didn't want Deangelo to hear.

"So how do you like Jasper?" CeCe asked.

Tamara looked up. "I've been here before, right? It's pretty much the same. Even the people. Same … people."

CeCe nodded and quickly sipped her water.

"Are we ready, ladies?" The *finally* was obvious in Lou's voice though he didn't say it as he walked back to us, his pad in his hand.

"We are." CeCe handed him back the menus and we quickly ordered a Meat Lovers Special for CeCe and half-Cheese, half-veggie for me. We liked to order extra so we each have leftovers for meals the next day. Or, in my case, for late-afternoon snacks.

As Lou started to walk away, CeCe jumped up and followed him. "Can we go ahead and pay for it now, please?"

Lou stopped, and I could swear he took a deep breath before he turned around. I'm pretty sure eye rolls were involved. "We typically take care of that at the end of your meal."

"We might need to run out quickly."

He stared at her, then shrugged. "Sure, let's take care of it now."

We both stepped over to the cashier and paid for our individual pizzas and drinks.

I tried to make conversation while we waited for Lou to ring us up. "At least I got veggies on mine this time instead of just cheese."

"You are going to start looking like cheese, you've eaten it so much lately." CeCe looked at me pointedly.

"I already look like cheese." I looked down at my slightly pudgy body. "Just without the holes."

A group of college students walked in and picked out seats. I growled a sigh of disgust. The lunch crowd already was beginning. Between Tamara and Deangelo and now the college kids, it would be harder for Lou to stop and talk with us about Jerry's murder.

We stood by the cashiers and waited for our drinks. As Lou handed them to us, I paused as I brought it to my mouth. "So, that was terrible about Jerry."

Lou froze and looked at me carefully. "Yeah, it was," he said shortly.

"Did he come in here a lot? I thought I saw him the other night after one of my yoga classes."

Lou gave a little chin nod. "Sometimes, he would hunker down in here."

"Didn't that bother you? I mean, he was clearly intoxicated the other night."

Lou gave the college students the "just a second" sign and leaned against the counter. "Why are you asking me about Jerry?"

CeCe and I looked at each other. "Because he was a small business owner like you and" she pointed to each of us. "Like us. It's a big deal."

Lou scoffed. "He wasn't a business owner. Sandy has been running that place single-handedly for the past 15 years. Not to speak ill of the dead-"

But now you're going to, I thought.

"But he was a drain on Sandy, financially, emotionally, physically, everything."

"You seem to know their situation pretty well." *Now we're getting somewhere.*

Lou shrugged. "Like you said, we're all small-business people, and they're just down the way from me. Sandy comes in a lot."

"How often did Jerry come in like that?"

"You mean drunk?"

I nodded.

He shrugged. "Three or four times a week."

"Order up!"

Lou's head jerked up and he started to turn.

"Are you having an affair with Sandy?" My eyes widened as CeCe blurted out the question that was most on our minds.

Lou froze, a stunned expression on his face. He peered hard at CeCe. "Why would you ask me a question like that?"

CeCe played with the condensation on the sides of her plastic cup. "Let's just say someone saw the two of you making googly eyes at each other one night."

His gaze ricocheted between CeCe and me. "Googly eyes? What are we, twelve?"

With that, he turned toward the kitchen, shaking his head as he went.

CeCe sipped on her straw. "That went well."

"Shut up."

Chapter 11

I stopped just outside the pizza place and sat down on a bench facing the door. CeCe looked around, then sat down beside me.

"Mariah, we have to get back to work." She waved a hand in front of my face, so I turned to face her. "We own businesses, remember?"

"Did you see the sparks fly between Tamara and Lou?"

She clutched her purse with one hand while holding onto her leftover pizza box with the other. "I saw them flirting. Is that what you mean?"

I nodded slowly. "It seemed like more than that. He fell all over himself to attend to her every little need."

CeCe nodded. "She's beautiful and exotic, Mariah. What's your point? I actually do need to get back to the shop."

"And *Paul*?" I sing-songed at her.

She smiled. "He's off today, though I hope to see him tonight. But especially when he's not there, I need to be there."

I crossed my arms. "Either one of them could have killed Jerry. It seems like they both had motive."

"Well, we'll just keep an eye on them, okay?"

I could tell she was just humoring me so I would stop talking. "Okay, your shop is closest to Luigi's, so you keep an eye on Lou. I'll keep watch on Tamara. If one of them is involved, we can take what we learn to Neil and spring Angelica from the pen."

"From the pen? Seriously?"

I laughed to myself. "I just always wanted to say that."

CeCe laughed with me and started to turn toward the street when the door to Luigi's sprang open, the handle banging against the wall behind it.

Deangelo bolted out, anger etched into his face. He stalked down the street and around the corner.

I turned to CeCe. "You go back to work. I'll go check on Tamara."

Without waiting for her reply, I scooted to the door, pausing to see if the handle was broken. Everything looked intact.

I walked back into the dimly lit restaurant and saw Tamara sitting alone at the table where we had left them.

I sat down beside her, settling my leftover pizza box on the table beside me.

"Everything all right, Tamara? We just saw Deangelo leave in a hurry."

She shrugged. "I'm fine. Deangelo is, well, he'll be fine, too. We're just dealing with some issues right now, you know, relationship things."

"How long have you been dating?"

"About six months."

"The story you two told the other night was sweet." I settled onto my chair to show I was interested, resisting the urge to check my watch to see how much time I had before my next private session appointment. "I love a good relationship story."

Tamara scoffed. "I don't know if ours is good or not, I mean, it's as good as any, right?" She quickly backpedaled when she saw my expression. "At least he doesn't ask me to go get coffee anymore."

"You don't like coffee?"

"Oh, never. I don't drink coffee. The caffeine in coffee is so bad for the spirit. It just really sucks the life out of our spiritual practice."

Huh. That's a new one. I didn't think it was a good time to mention my own caffeine habit. By the way, I was starting to crave a mocha. Maybe I would try it with coconut milk instead of almond milk this time, or perhaps just go full on whole milk for a change. My mind started to consider the possibilities, including perhaps a shot of caramel flavoring--

"Mariah?" Tamara smiled indulgently. "You looked like you went somewhere else."

I caught myself licking my lips and wondering if I should mention that my favorite place next to my studio, was CeCe's coffee shop. I decided to keep my mouth shut.

"Sorry, my mind wandered. Tell me more about you and Deangelo."

Apparently the two of them went to a tea shop instead and have been inseparable ever since.

"And how do you know his sister, Angelica?"

"She is such a sweetie. We met at the hospital where I was teaching yoga. She was doing some kind of, I don't know, program there."

"EMT."

"Excuse me?"

"She's studying to be an EMT, emergency medical technician."

"Oh, right. Sometimes I am so flaky. Of course, she's training to be an EMT. She'll be really good at it." Tamara shook her head and twirled her water glass. "Mostly she and I talk about yoga and the work she does for me, and, of course, recovery. It's so vital for former addicts, right?"

"Right." Tamara's pizza showed up just then. Lou insisted on serving her the first piece, setting the plate in front of her. He looked around for Deangelo. She silently waved his gaze back to her.

"He had to leave. We can just wrap up his half of the pizza."

"Sure, no worries. How about I keep you company then?" Lou sat down across from Tamara and looked at me. "Don't you have a class or something?"

I looked purposely at my watch. "I have time."

Tamara giggled. "It's fine, Mariah. I am in Lou's safe hands."

I knew when I had been dismissed. I stood up and walked toward the door. When I looked back, Lou was taking a bite from the pizza on Deangelo's side.

Chapter 12

I mulled over this new information as I walked down Main Street toward The Yoga Mat, then stopped in my yoga-shod tracks, staring toward the diner. Neil Samuelson walked with a blond woman across the street from me. I stopped behind a light pole and peeked at them.

He walked on the side nearest the road, as any small-town gentleman would, so his face was turned away from mine. The woman was pretty, with long hair, a skirt that was just this side of office-appropriate and a tight-fitting top. Not that I was judging. She laughed at something he said and touched his arm lightly. He leaned in to hear her response. I could hear her laughter from my spot behind the pole.

Someone bumped into me, knocking me awry and nearly knocking the pizza from my hands.

"Mariah, I'm so sorry. Are you okay?" I looked up to see CeCe's barista, Paul, a smile on his face and a bag of groceries in his hand.

"No worries. Are you cooking tonight?" I motioned to the bag in his hand.

"Nothing fancy. Chicken alfredo with a salad." He looked at me uncertainly for a moment. "Do you think CeCe will like it?"

I paused. Should I mess with him or not? He seemed so earnest, I decided not to. I nodded vigorously. "She'll love it, especially if there is something yummy for dessert."

Paul held up the bag. "Strawberries with cream."

"Perfect." I started to turn away, casting my eyes back across the street.

"What are you doing?" He looked across the street at Neil and the blond, who had reached the door of the diner. "Because it looks like you're stalking someone."

We both watched as Neil opened the door and the woman entered the diner before him.

I harrumphed and stood up a little straighter.

"I'm not a stalker. Don't believe everything CeCe tells you. I'm going back to work now. I have a business to run." Then I turned and continued walking toward The Yoga Mat but not before I saw a smile flicker across Paul's face. *Dang it. He'd probably rat me out to CeCe, too.*

Who was that blond woman? I didn't remember seeing her in town and was sure she hadn't been in any of my yoga classes. Were they dating? I had thought he was interested in me. He did seem to come around here a lot.

"What the heck?" The words meant only for myself flew out of my mouth as I swung open the door of The Yoga Mat, belatedly remembering that Cindy's noon class was just finishing.

I peeked over the double saloon doors that separated the lobby from the studio. Cindy sat on her mat at the front of the class, while her students lay flat on their mats in *savasana*, at least the ones who didn't open their eyes to see who had interrupted their meditation time. I stood on my tiptoes and mouthed the words "I'm sorry" over the doors. Cindy just smiled and waved me away.

I stepped quietly into my office, slipping off my shoes just inside, then closed the door before I turned on my light so I wouldn't further disturb the students. Only a few minutes remained before Cindy and her students would be filling the lobby with chatter, so I quickly pulled out student lists and receipts. Stormy did a great job of organizing everything, so all I had to do was match the receipts with the bank balance on my laptop. I happily noticed that the bank balance had continued its upward trajectory.

Cindy rang a chime signaling the end of *savasana* and students began to move around. I heard her end the class with an inspirational quote that I found cheesy, but students seemed to like it.

Cindy hooked open the saloon doors on the sides with a click, then stuck her head in the office.

"Hey, boss."

I looked up and smiled. Cindy was my big sister and sheriff in the county. But at The Yoga Mat, I was the boss. It was a good feeling and Cindy knew it. Having her teach a noon class was dicey at times, because occasionally the bad guys did their deeds in broad daylight.

Every once in a while, I would get an urgent text saying she couldn't teach that day. I was so grateful for her help at the studio that I didn't mind.

Truth be told, I would spend every waking hour at The Yoga Mat if I could. Cindy had convinced me it would be bad for my sanity to be here constantly, so she had gotten certified to teach last year when I was first planning to move to Jasper.

"How was class?"

She shrugged. "Good as any. How was lunch?"

I held up the box of leftover pizza. "Good as any. Want some pizza?"

She laughed and shook her head, then reached over her head to adjust the high ponytail she always wore in yoga and to work. "More pizza? I still have leftovers from the other night in the fridge at the station. I'm going to go back and heat them up. Charlie is pizza-ed out and doesn't want me to bring it home for dinner."

I smiled at her husband's assessment. He was more a meat and potatoes guy.

Cindy said goodbye to the last of the noon students, then reached to snag her satchel from behind the office door so she could change before going back to the post. "I might see if Neil wants some pizza."

"He's already eaten."

Cindy's hand froze over the satchel and her eyes met mine. "And you would know this how? Anything you'd like to share, little sister?"

I shook my head and looked down at the papers in my hand, pretending they were super important. "I just happen to see him and some blonde go into the diner a little bit ago, that's all."

"Some blonde?" Cindy's hand continued its descent. She picked up the satchel, then paused. "Long hair, short skirt?"

"That's the one." I refused to take my eyes off my pretend-important papers.

"It's probably Lindsay Carlton. Paralegal at the courthouse. She dates every single man in town at some point or other. I wouldn't worry."

With that, she slipped out the office door and into the studio's bathroom to change.

"I'm not worried." I knew I was speaking to myself. I rustled the papers in my hands. "What do I have to be worried about? It's not like we're dating. Not worried even a little bit."

The front door slid open and Jennifer Parks stepped quietly inside as I tucked the papers back into the binder and with a shove, stuck the whole binder back on the shelf.

She jumped a little. "That was forceful."

"Oh, hi, Jennifer. Can I help you?"

"I just wanted to stop by to talk about the next fundraiser."

I invited her into my office, opening one of the folding metal chairs for her to sit on. She pulled out her calendar and a folder. As she was tapping on her phone to get to her calendar, I remembered seeing her with Jerry the morning of his death.

"How are you feeling? I know you were upset about Jerry McIntyre."

Jennifer's eyes shot upward and she hesitated.

"Yes, it was sad. I'm sorry I got so bent out of shape at the diner yesterday."

"Did you know him well?"

She scrunched her face as if remembering. "I suppose as well as anyone. He was my cousin, you know. Well, second cousin."

Well, now there's some new information. "No, I didn't know. I'm so sorry for your loss. I thought you said he was a friend?"

Jennifer shrugged, keeping her eyes on the phone in her hand. "It's all right. He had a lot of struggles in his life, and, yes, he was a friend. I mean, I thought of him more as a friend than a relative."

I looked up to see Cindy wave as she headed out the front door, now dressed in her sheriff's uniform.

I decided to try Cindy's trick of waiting for someone to speak as I put my eyes back on Jennifer. She kept hers on the folders in her hand. As the silence dragged on a beat too long, Jennifer spoke quietly, her voice increasing in urgency.

"He wasn't a bad man, you know. He still had a lot to give the world. I hate hearing everyone talk about how he was the town drunk. He wasn't! He was an alcoholic and people should have more compassion."

Surprised by the forcefulness of her response, I tried to figure out where to go with questioning. I didn't want to waste this opportunity. "Did the Sheriff's deputies question you about his murder?"

Her eyes flew to mine. "Why would they question me? I had nothing to do with it."

"They've questioned a lot of people. You being a relative and all, maybe you could give them information." I sat back in my chair, my eyes riveted on Jennifer's face. "Plus, I did notice the two of you having an argument that day in the Mercantile. Did you tell the deputies about that?"

Jennifer's eyes narrowed. "Why would I tell them about that? It was just a disagreement. It had nothing to do with Jerry's murder."

Her mouth fell open. "Wait a minute. You think I killed my cousin? Why would I do that?"

She stood up shoving her papers back into her bag. "I cannot believe you, Mariah. Just because you figured out Patricia's killer does not give you license to go around accusing people of Jerry's murder."

"You don't want to tell me?"

"No!"

With that, Jennifer turned and stalked out of the studio. Maybe we wouldn't be having a Safety Blanket fundraiser after all.

After she left, I plopped back into the chair at my desk. Jennifer was Jerry's cousin. Was there more about her that I didn't know? Was there more about Jerry's death that she did know?

I hopped from my chair and slipped into the studio, then spread out my mat and sat down softly, moving through some seated stretches. I just needed some quiet time to sift through the information about the murder and what I'd learned from Jennifer. I did *not* need quiet time to mull over what Detective Neil Samuelson was up to right now.

Reaching my hands overhead, I leaned toward the right, letting my hands follow. It's just that I had kind of thought he was interested in me. It had been a long time since I'd been interested in another man, and, well, yes, I was definitely attracted to him. *There*, I'd said it to myself, if not exactly out loud. It's not as if I had sworn off men after my divorce, but Lee and I had been married almost fifteen years, and I was … cautious … about another relationship. Cautious? Perhaps, wary, nervous, anxious. Okay, I admit it. I was scared.

Inhaling, I returned to a seated position, then began to exhale and folded to the other side. Well, fine, if he is interested in someone else, *fine*. I have more important things to think about than a detective who insists on arresting me and my friends. After all, I have a new business to–

Josie burst through the studio doors before I could finish my thought. "Mariah, I have another clue!"

I stretched both hands over my head, then exhaled them together to my chest before I looked up to answer her.

"Whatcha got?"

She stepped on the back of each foot to take off her shoes, then scurried into the studio. I moved to one end of my mat and motioned for her to sit on the other.

"I overheard Neil and Cindy talking about something they found on Jerry's body. It was a stone."

I pumped a fist. "I knew there was more to that rock than Neil told me."

Puzzlement covered Josie's face, so I filled her in on the small red rock that I had found at the crime scene, the one Neil had seemed sure wasn't related to the case. I won't lie, I smirked a little inside.

Josie nodded in agreement. "Apparently, another small Jasper stone was found inside the collar on Jerry's shirt." She lifted up the collar on her uniform to show me. "Neil said it must have fallen in after Jerry fell down because otherwise it would have fallen out long before."

Josie leaned closer. "But not just any Jasper."

My eyebrows went up on their own. Apparently, even they couldn't wait to hear what was about to come next.

"It was Red Jasper."

I took a breath and tried to focus my thoughts around this new information. "Lots of people carry Jasper, especially around here," I pointed out. "Where does someone get Jasper around here, besides from their sister?"

"That's the problem. You can get Jasper pretty much anywhere. You can buy it at the Corner Mercantile or other stores. You can find Jasper in the river. It's fairly common, so it's not worth much."

"Do you think most people know the spiritual significance of Red Jasper, or do they just think it's pretty?"

Josie shrugged. "I would err on the side of most folks just thinking it's pretty, except for your students. I've heard you talk about it in class sometimes."

I mulled that over. "But if it ended up in Jerry's collar upside down, it got there after he fell to the ground and that means–."

Josie and I locked eyes. "–the killer carried the Red Jasper."

Chapter 13

Josie and I decided to find out where Red Jasper was available in town. I hated the idea that one of my students might have dropped the stone because – arghh! – that would mean yet another student was a killer.

I was pretty sure I'd seen the stones at the Corner Mercantile, and Josie thought she had seen it in the little jewelry store tucked in next to Luigi's. Josie stayed for class, somewhat against her wishes, so afterward, we set off, leaving Stormy to watch the studio.

She frowned at me as we put on our shoes. "So now that I work for you, I don't get to help solve murders?"

Josie and I exchanged a quick glance, and I accidentally slipped my shoes on the wrong feet. I ducked my head as I bent down to fix them and figure out what to say. Stormy had been a huge help when I was accused of murder last month, but mostly because I thought she might have done it and she thought I had done it. She had been doing exactly what I had been doing – trying to make sure she didn't go to jail and ready to throw me under the bus to save herself.

Still, we'd grown closer since she started working at The Yoga Mat and I didn't want to hurt her feelings.

Once more, honesty seemed the best route, if I was going to practice *satya*, and I was, I really was. I lifted my head from my shoes.

"Stormy, right now, we're just going to check out the shops that sell it. It's more helpful to me if you mind the studio while I'm gone."

Stormy casually checked out her fingernails, which were always perfect, so I knew she was just doing it for effect. "What if I told you I know where to get Red Jasper?"

Josie and I sat up a little straighter and peered at Stormy.

"Where?"

"How?"

Josie's tone was a lot more accusatory than mine, like the deputy she was.

Stormy shrugged. "My little brother and I used to find Red J in the river, clean it up and sell it around town. You don't think those snooty shop owners dig it up themselves, do you?" She straightened the sign-in sheet at the front counter, then turned to go back into the office, calling from inside. "But hey, if you don't need my help, that's fine by me. I have work to do."

Josie and I sat back in the lobby chairs, smiling. I stood up and went to the office door. "Okay, how about a compromise? We'll go snoop around the shops. Tomorrow after class, you can take Josie and me down to the river to show us where you and your brother found the Red Jasper."

Stormy flipped open the laptop on top of the desk and sat down. "Sounds like a plan." She grinned as she sat down, throwing me a glance. "Thanks, boss."

Chapter 14

Josie turned in one direction while I headed down the street toward the Corner Mercantile. I paused to let a car out of the alley and realized I had no plan for finding out information at the Corner Mercantile. I knew it was one of the main shops that sold Red Jasper, but I couldn't very well ask Sandy if she had sold it to the killer. I sat down on the street-side bench and closed my eyes to concentrate.

It occurred to me that I needed a few more things for my Movie Night basket. I could use that as my reason for stopping in at the Corner Mercantile. I smiled to myself at my own quick thinking. Many of the local shop owners were tired of coming up with basket themes every month for the silent auction, but I was still new enough that I found it fun. Besides, we only had a couple more months before the City Council had raised enough money for the big Jasper Days festivities, which I was eagerly awaiting. I had arrived just after last year's celebration, so I didn't know exactly what to expect.

Suddenly I felt someone next to me. My eyes flew open as I jumped.

Neil Samuelson laughed lightly as he sat down beside me. "You're mighty jumpy, Ms. Stevens."

I turned toward him as my heart rate couldn't decide if it should settle down or pitter-patter like crazy. My voice was calmer than I expected it to be. "There's a killer on the loose, Detective Samuelson. Of course, I'm jumpy."

"What if I told you I had the killer in jail?" He leaned against the back of the seat and stretched out his long legs, then dug into a white bag he was carrying and pulled out a sugar-coated doughnut. He broke it in half and offered one to me.

I stared at it. "You're eating a doughnut? Didn't you just have lunch?"

"A while ago. How did you know?" He turned to stare at me, his eyebrows raised.

I looked away and settled back on the bench. "I saw you go into the diner."

Silence. I peeked out of the corner of my eye to see Neil biting his lip. *Aha!* He knew that I had seen him with the blonde.

"Yeah, but it wasn't a great lunch, so I kept it as short as I could. Sure you don't want this?"

He waved the doughnut under my nose. I could practically taste the cinnamon sugar on top. I was tempted to refuse, but only for a second, so I accepted with a slight bow, then settled back on the bench next to him. My insides were doing a happy dance with the news that lunch with Blondie was a bomb. I felt oddly nervous now that I had admitted to myself that I was attracted to the detective.

"For a yoga teacher, you sure have a terrible diet."

"You're not the first person to notice that."

He smiled as he looked over at me and threw an arm over the back of the bench as he munched his half of the doughnut. "I actually kind of like that you're not one of those super-skinny, super-flexible yoga teachers. It makes yoga seem more reachable, even a non-flexible guy like me can do it."

"Yeah, sure, that's why I eat doughnuts, so my students and local law enforcement can feel better about themselves."

"Ooh, do I detect sarcasm?"

I shoved the rest of the doughnut into my mouth so I wouldn't have to answer. Then I slowly licked some of the sugar off my fingers before wiping the rest on my yoga pants before I could catch myself. Hopefully, my students wouldn't be close enough to me to smell cinnamon sugar doughnut on my pants.

When I finished, I turned back to Neil and changed the subject. I didn't really want to keep talking about how not-skinny I was.

"Detective, you don't have the right person in jail. I can just feel it."

He looked me in the eyes, his gaze softening. "I can't solve a case on gut feeling alone, Mariah. I have to follow the evidence."

"*I have to follow the evidence.* You always say that."

"Because it's true. It's not quick and easy like on TV. It's painstaking, and unfortunately, that makes it painful for the other people involved." He sat up and brushed his hands together to sweep off the sugar. "Mariah, please don't get mad at me again for doing my job."

I brushed the sugar off my yoga pants and stood up, pausing to look at him. "It is painful. I can't help being mad at you. But if you need evidence, then I'll find your evidence."

He blew out a breath and looked toward the sky as I picked up my reusable shopping bag. "Mariah-"

"See you later, Detective. Thanks for the doughnut."

I walked quickly away before he could stop me. Now my walk had a purpose. As I strode past the Corner Mercantile, I could see Sandy at the cashier's counter. I waved as I entered the store, then snagged a basket and moved down an aisle. I picked up some colorful paper and ribbons, then turned toward the end of the counter, where the Red Jasper and other stones were kept in boxes.

As Sandy checked through a customer, they chatted about the upcoming Movie Night. I picked up the rocks and looked through them, feeling their smoothness and letting them fall through my fingers. It would be easy for someone to steal one when Sandy's back was turned.

"Looking for anything in particular, Mariah?" Sandy appeared practically at my elbow. I startled, dropping the stone I was looking at back in the pile.

I shook my head. "I was thinking of putting some Red Jasper in my Movie Night basket for the Silent Auction this month."

"Why would you want to do that? They're pretty common around here."

Sandy looked puzzled as she moved back to her side of the counter. She reached into the lapel pocket of her smock and pulled out a handful of stones, which she dropped on the counter. Some of the stones were red, others blue and green. "You can dig up all kinds of stones like this at the river."

"I've heard that. I'm surprised more people don't do it. I was thinking of digging up some myself."

Sandy gave me a mock frown, then smiled so I would know she was kidding. "Now don't go taking all my business, Mariah. Like I said, most aren't very valuable. But still, don't go blabbing about finding them in the river." She waved a hand over the boxes of rocks on the counter. "I don't make a ton of money from them, but it's enough to make it worthwhile."

I played with the rock in my hand and tried to figure out how to get out of this conversation. "I thought I might glue the rock to a card that told about its properties. That might make it special."

"What properties?"

"I talk about it in my classes sometimes. Red Jasper is said to increase passion and help restore justice when an injustice has been done."

"You don't say. They increase passion?" Sandy stared at the rock in her hand.

I placed the rock back in the box. These rocks were clean and shiny, unlike the one that I had seen at the crime scene. "I'll give it some thought. How do you keep shoplifters from taking the rocks?"

Sandy nodded as she made a face. "Sometimes kids will pinch a few, but I think they're common enough that no one takes them. You ready?" She motioned toward the cashier's counter.

I placed my items on the counter and started to dig into my purse. Glancing up, I paused and looked toward the back of the store, where the door of the storeroom was open. Sure enough, I could easily see into the room from the cashier's stand. Apparently, Sandy's alibi was sound.

Sandy cleared her throat and I pulled my gaze away from the back door. "Have you heard anything more about my husband's killer?"

She didn't look at me, just kept checking through the groceries.

I nearly dropped my purse in surprise. "I'm not sure, I mean, how would I know?"

She kept her eyes on the cash register. "Well, your sister is the sheriff. The sheriff's office hasn't been very helpful. I keep calling and they tell me they have a person of interest and that they're working on it. Plus, I've heard that you and that CeCe are poking around again, like you did when they thought you killed that woman. I thought they had someone in jail and the case was solved, so I was confused when I heard the rumors about you and CeCe."

Sandy finished putting my supplies in the cloth shopping bag I had handed her. She looked up at me with what seemed to be tears in her eyes. "It won't bring him back, but I sure would like to know who did it."

A new voice broke in. "We all would, Mrs. McIntyre."

I briefly closed my eyes when I heard Maya Anderson's voice. How did she keep sneaking up on me like this? I hadn't even heard the front doorbell ding.

I ignored the reporter as I reached out and gently touched Sandy's hand.

"Me, too, Sandy. I don't know what to say. I don't think Angelica Vazquez killed your husband, but I don't know who did. If I can help find the person responsible, I want to help. Take care of yourself. You know you have a standing offer of yoga at The Yoga Mat."

I smiled as I released her hand and reached for my bag.

Sandy was reaching for a tissue as I left the store, throwing a glare over my shoulder toward Maya. I wondered how long she had been standing there. Did she hear our conversation?

Maya focused her eyes on Sandy. The store owner took a deep breath, then lifted her head as if she could shake off all of her troubles.

Poor woman. Sandy might not be the easiest person to deal with, but she had been dealt a tough hand in life.

The bad news was that if Sandy had heard that CeCe and I were helping Josie, then surely Neil and Cindy had heard it, too, and that did not bode well for me. But I had given Josie my word and I intended to stand by that.

As I marched toward The Yoga Mat, Josie's brother, Deangelo, struggled out of the hardware store, arms full of paint and supplies. I hurried toward him.

"Can I give you a hand, Deangelo?"

Josie's brother's face was etched with a frown as he peeked over the top of his purchases. When he saw it was me, a weak smile appeared.

"Can you grab my truck key? It's in my jeans pocket."

I backed up and stared at him, holding out my hand like a stop sign. "Whoa, dude. You really want me to go digging around in your pants pocket in the middle of Main Street? You do know your sister is law enforcement, right? And so is mine, for that matter."

Deangelo's cheeks flushed and then he started to laugh. "Maybe just hold this stuff in my right hand and I'll get the key?"

I reached out and grabbed the bag with one hand, still holding on to my own bag with the other. Deangelo quickly hit the button to unlock the doors and turned back to take the bag, which I appreciated because it was heavier than it looked.

"Thank you, Mariah." Deangelo turned back to me after getting everything situated in the passenger seat of the truck.

"Looks like you have some projects ahead of you."

He nodded and smiled sadly, his dark eyes crinkling in his handsome face. "You bet. That's why Tamara and I came up early before your workshop. I wanted to help Mama take care of some things around the house. Josie and Sammy help her out with the day-to-day chores, but sometimes, those bigger projects pile up."

I patted his arm and smiled. "I know your mom appreciates it and is so glad you're home for a while."

He laughed ruefully, shaking his head. "It sure hasn't turned out like we thought it would."

"Deangelo," I wasn't sure if I should broach the subject or not. "Why would Neil, I mean, Detective Samuelson be keeping Angelica in jail?"

He raised his hand as if to ward off questions. "I don't know. Something about protecting Tamara. Not that she needs protecting."

"Did she ever talk about what happened to her when she was a kid here, why she left early that one summer?"

I wasn't sure Deangelo would answer. His eyes searched my face, as if he was looking for a sign as to how I would respond. I tried to look sympathetic, which I was, so it wasn't difficult. Finally, he spoke.

"Yeah, she did. But not until we got back together in L.A. I finally asked her why she had left. You know, she broke my heart pretty bad back then. I couldn't figure out why she just left and didn't tell me goodbye or anything."

"Did you believe her?"

He looked stricken – and angry. "Of course! Nobody makes up stuff like that. It took years for her to heal from it."

"So you were angry at Jerry McIntyre?"

Deangelo slammed shut the open door, rattling the truck to its rims before he answered. His eyes were dark as he looked at me, taking a step closer. I stepped back.

"Of course, I was angry. Who wouldn't be? Are you interrogating me, Mariah? Is that what's going on here?" He stepped closer, shoving his pointer finger in my face. "I was so angry I could have killed him. Is that what you want to hear? Well, it's true. I was that angry. But I didn't kill him, and neither did Angelica and neither did Tamara."

He backed up, shaking his head and reached for the door handle without looking at me. "If you weren't a friend of Josie's…"

His voice trailed off, apparently deciding more words was not the way to go. Pulling his keys back out of his jeans pocket, he wrenched open the truck door and leaped onto the seat. I stepped back on the sidewalk and watched him leave.

Deangelo was angry enough to kill and, judging by how easily he had jumped up onto that seat, he was strong enough to do it, too.

"Mariah, wait up!"

My heart sank as Maya Anderson called my name from across the street. She looked both ways, then trotted toward me.

"Hey, Maya. What's up?"

"Just wondering if you had any new leads in Jerry's murder." She re-situated her bag and pulled out her notebook, looking at me expectantly.

"Do I look like a Sheriff's deputy?" I tried, but I just couldn't keep the sarcasm out of my voice.

Maya's face creased as she smiled. "Now, Mariah, I know you're helping Josie try to get Angelica off. Tough gig, if you ask me."

"I didn't." My voice was colder than I wanted it to be. I couldn't afford to alienate Maya. "There are suspects everywhere, you know. For instance, I was wondering how it was that you knew Jerry was dead before he actually was. I mean, the ambulance was taking him away."

Maya stared at me and sputtered. "I didn't know. I mean, how could I?"

"That's right. How could you know?"

She looked at me a moment too long. "I'm not sure I like what you're insinuating, Mariah. Why would I want Jerry dead?"

I shrugged. "You and Jennifer Parks are close, and she seems pretty broken up about it."

"Because Jerry's dead, not because I killed him." Maya leaned in close to my face. "Be careful who you are accusing, Mariah. Some of us might not take it too kindly."

Then she turned and stepped quickly across the street. I blew out a breath I didn't know I was holding and stared after her. We might have to look into Maya Anderson a bit more carefully.

I started to step into The Yoga Mat, then remembered Stormy was there. What I wanted was quiet. Or information. Or both. What was I missing? How did Neil do this day after day without his head exploding?

Perhaps a visit to Angelica was in order. I didn't want to embarrass her by visiting her in jail, but I needed more information.

Checking my watch to make sure I was good on time, I turned away from the studio and headed down the street. The Sheriff's

Department was at the other end of Main Street, on the edge of downtown. That way, officers could easily access the freeway and other roads to reach the nearby towns they served. We were lucky to have the post in Jasper, besides the fact that my sister was the boss there.

I was sweating when I reached the big gray building containing the Sheriff's Department as well as other law enforcement agencies and the county jail. Josie sat at the front desk behind the bullet-proof glass.

"Yes, ma'am," she said into the microphone. "How may I help you?" Then she made a face at me.

I laughed. "I came to see Angelica."

Josie nodded and checked the schedule on the clipboard by her elbow. She pressed a button to open the door and let me in.

"I'll take you back." She motioned to the other deputy at the desk, who was on the phone but nodded in response. Following Josie through the dark narrow hallway brought back unpleasant memories. My arms scrunched to my sides, a chill went up my back as I remembered walking this same hallway last month when I had been accused of murdering my student. I shivered involuntarily.

Josie leaned toward me as we walked.

"Any luck with the Red Jasper?" Her voice was barely a whisper.

I shook my head. "They sit out on the counter in the boxes. Anyone could take them. But Sandy seemed upset about Jerry."

"Understandable. It's only been a couple of days."

"How about you?" I asked.

Josie shrugged. "About the same. A couple of the stores sell them, but it seems like they all get them from Sandy."

We stepped through the door at the end of the hallway.

Angelica was in her cell, moving. I smiled as I recognized Sun Salutations, a flow that helps to ground the practitioner and promote strength. She lifted her hips into Downward Dog as the door clanged shut behind us. With a grin at us beneath her arm pit, she then effortlessly swung first one foot and then the other into a standing position. Bringing her hands to her heart in a prayer position to "seal" her practice, she smiled again and stepped to the bars.

Josie blew a kiss to her sister but stayed by the door, her hands at her side, near her gun.

"Protocol," she said plainly. "I have to stay where the camera can see me."

I turned back to Angelica. "You don't seem to be doing too badly in here."

She smiled and pointed to an aluminum foil-wrapped package. "I'm getting Mama's fresh tamales. It's almost worth it to be in here." She smiled broadly and then chuckled, her face softening. "This is not my first rodeo, Mariah. However, it is the first one when I've been clean and sober and, oh, yeah, actually *did not* do what they're accusing me of. I feel oddly relaxed about it."

"Seriously?" I stared at her in amazement. "When I was in here, I was a basket case."

"Yeah, but you were also in here with a drunken miscreant." Josie joined in the conversation from across the room.

I looked over at the cell where he had been. "That's true enough. But still. How are you really doing?"

Angelica held up her hands. "I am surprisingly not worried. I figure it like this: If they got the right person when they arrested me all those times before, then they'll get the right person again." She leaned toward me and lowered her voice. "Besides, there were an awful lot of times I should have gotten arrested but didn't, so I figure it's a little bit of karma going around."

"I heard that." Josie spoke up again, and we all laughed.

"Angelica," I tried to get serious with the young woman before me. "Why would they think you killed Jerry, besides the fact that you were holding the knife?"

Angelica took a deep breath and stepped closer to me and the bars. Her voice was quiet. "I had a slip a year or so ago, not a big one. I was at a party with some friends and my boyfriend was flirting with some girl, and I got mad and drank a little Jack Daniels."

"How much is a little?"

Angelica grimaced. "A fifth."

Oh.

"I was out of commission for a day or two while I recovered and Tamara helped cover for me at the hospital program because I missed a couple of days."

"Did she know why?"

Angelica nodded. "She was really understanding, but she said she would only help me this one slip. The next time it happened, she wouldn't help me."

"That's harsh."

"It's what I needed at the time. I came back to recovery and threw myself into it all. I owe Tamara so much."

Realization dawned and I stepped closer to the cell, putting my hands on the bars.

"Back away from the cell, Mariah."

I recoiled from the cell at Josie's sharp words, glancing over at her. "Dang, deputy, that's harsh, too."

She shrugged. "How do I know you're not passing her something?"

"Anyway…" I turned back to Angelica. "So, the Sheriff's detective thinks you would do anything to help Tamara, including taking revenge on Jerry?"

Angelica nodded.

I took a breath and glanced back at Josie, who looked like she wasn't listening, but who apparently hadn't missed a thing.

"Would you?" I asked. "Would you do anything for Tamara?"

Angelica thought for a moment, her hand playing with her long ponytail, then shook her head. "I would do a lot, but I wouldn't break the law and I definitely wouldn't kill for her. It would mess me up so much inside that I'd probably drink and use again. I got off easy this time, with just a fifth of whisky. I might not be so lucky next time."

She paused, pulling her hands to the back of her head and readjusting her ponytail, which seemed a little too perky for the Jasper County Jail.

"Besides, I kind of feel that I've nearly paid her back for all her help and was thinking of quitting when we got back to LA. I need to focus on my studies for my final semester."

I pursed my lips and studied Angelica. No matter what Neil said, not one single vibe from Angelica screamed, "I'm a killer!"

"Where were you before you showed up at the hotel?"

"I was at the house, helping Mama make sopapillas. They're my favorite."

I involuntarily licked my lips. I'd heard about her Mama's baking. "Are there any left?"

She smiled. "Probably not, Mariah, but I bet Mama would make you some more."

I shook myself out of my food detour. "What made you come to the hotel that night?"

"Tamara called and asked me to come at seven o'clock."

"She said specifically seven? Did she say why?"

Angelica shrugged. "I think she was going to dinner or something beforehand, but she would be done by seven, she said."

My face screwed up at that. How could Tamara have already gone to dinner when she and Deangelo were just leaving right after the police arrived? The timing seemed wrong.

With that, I said my goodbyes, gazed longingly at the tamales, then Josie and I turned and left the room. If I were the suspicious type, I would wonder why Tamara wanted Angelica to show up at a specific time and then lie about the reason. Could it be coincidence that a dead man greeted Angelica, or was Tamara trying to hide something?

Chapter 15

Cindy waited for me when I walked out of the dim hallway. I wasn't surprised. Word travels fast at the Sheriff's post.

I nodded to her. "Sheriff."

"Little sister." She waited, giving me that little head tilt with the questioning eyes that read "I know you've been up to something." She had great wait time. "Anything you want to tell me?"

I shrugged. "I was visiting Angelica. She's been helping set up Tamara's workshop."

"Uh-huh. Is that all?"

I held up my hands palms-up in the international sign of "I'm innocent. What more could there be?"

Cindy laughed and shook her head. "Anyway, got time for an early dinner?"

I glanced at the big round clock on the wall and realized I was starving. That half-doughnut did not hold me through the afternoon. I agreed, and we headed out the door with a wave to Josie.

Once we had settled into our booth at the diner, sipping our respective ice teas, Cindy closed her menu and looked at me across the table.

"I know Josie asked you to help clear Angelica."

"Why would you think that?" I was almost positive Josie had not told her boss she had asked an amateur sleuth to poke around in the case.

Cindy rolled her eyes and looked at the ceiling for a moment. "Do you really think I'm so bad at my job that I don't know these things? I know Josie well and I know you well and I know people all over town who tell me things." She paused and sipped her water. "Did you learn anything from visiting Angelica?"

"I learned that Angelica is far too level-headed to have stabbed a man she had barely seen in a decade."

Cindy shrugged and nodded at the same time, being as noncommittal as possible. "Even though she was standing over the victim with the murder weapon in her hand?"

"Yes, even then. There must be some way forensics can show she came to the scene late?"

Cindy silently applauded with both hands. I couldn't tell if she was being sarcastic or not. "Nice sleuthing, sis. Forensics data does indicate that there would have been blood splatters on Angelica's t-shirt."

"Were there any?"

She shook her head. "There were some smudges at the bottom of her T-shirt, which would track with her leaning into the body to grab the knife."

"Well, that's something."

"It's not conclusive, however."

"Cindy, Angelica didn't have a motive. She told me she wouldn't kill for someone else, even Tamara."

"Even though Tamara had bailed her out before, literally?"

"Even then."

"She did say that Tamara asked her to come to the hotel by the back way promptly at seven o'clock."

"Yes, we knew that, too."

"So, I was wondering if Tamara might have set her up."

"Why would Tamara want Jerry dead?"

I looked at her in surprise. "If I've heard the rumors, surely you have? I mean, you were here when it happened."

"I was here, and I talked to Sandy. She said it never happened."

"And you believe her?"

Cindy played with her water glass. "Who would you believe? The woo-woo yoga goddess or the wife of the victim and an upright citizen never in a moment's trouble?"

I sighed in frustration. "Why don't people ever believe women?"

"Mariah, they're both women."

"Yes, but you're believing the scenario that is easier for you instead of the one where a man might have hurt a girl."

Cindy sucked in her lower lip, usually a sign that she was thinking through something. She blew out a breath and slowly nodded. "I could see where it might look that way."

Bev stopped over just then to take our orders. Cindy chose the chicken with au gratin potatoes. I paused before I ordered. The potatoes sounded good. I went for the potatoes with broccoli.

"Are you sure you're getting enough protein ordering that?"

I can't even count the number of times well-meaning friends and even strangers have asked me that question since I quit eating meat. I resisted the urge to roll my eyes and blast Cindy, even though she had questioned me about my eating habits many times before.

I smiled patiently on the outside. "The average potato has about four grams of protein. The average serving of broccoli has, I think, about the same. About four grams. That's already eight grams of protein right there."

Cindy smirked. "I can do the math, thank you. But the daily requirements, as I recall, are about fifty grams daily for an average woman."

I leaned back to look at her. "Ooh, look who's been studying up on nutrition." I took another sip of my tea. "Well, I also ate a container of yogurt today, which had about seventeen grams of protein."

"Yippee, now you're up to twenty-five, still only halfway." Cindy smiled triumphantly.

I sat back and wracked my brain. I knew I had eaten enough protein, but I couldn't remember exactly. Besides, I figured that high-protein days balanced out lower-protein days.

"I had some soup," I said slowly. "I know there was protein in there." I shrugged my shoulders. "I can't add it all up today, but I will review my diet and make sure I'm getting enough protein. Are you satisfied?"

Cindy nodded, a superior smile on her face. Bev chose that time to set our plates down in front of us, so we picked up our forks and dove in.

I reached for a buttered roll from the basket on the table and held one up like a prize. "Aha! Protein! There's protein in bread, more than you might think, in fact. So there."

Cindy just laughed, bit off some chicken and made loud eating sounds. Once we had comfortably eaten for a while, she wiped her mouth with her napkin and placed it back on her lap.

"Anyway, about Angelica?"

"Cindy, I just want to help."

"Mariah, we are working this case. Right now, the evidence leads to Angelica. Please let us follow the evidence without getting in the way."

I really wanted to say something, but the look on Cindy's face convinced me otherwise. I quickly stabbed another piece of broccoli and shoved it in my mouth before I was tempted.

"Good choice," Cindy murmured, turning her attention back to her plate.

Sometimes I wish she didn't know me so well.

As we left the diner, Cindy walked me back to the studio. In the office, I rummaged through my desk for next month's schedule. We were trading a couple of classes next month since she had some conflicts with her sheriff's duties.

Finally, I smacked my head with my hand. "Wait a sec. It's in the car. I typed it up at home last night."

We stepped around the edges of the studio so we didn't have to remove our shoes. I'm usually a stickler about that, but I was ready to get home, so I let it slide. Heading out the back door, I used the key fob to unlock the doors and started to open the passenger side, where I'd tossed the schedule on the seat.

"Mariah, wait."

Something about Cindy's voice made me stop and look back at her. She pointed to my car and we silently walked around it. All four tires were flat, with big gashes in the sides.

Someone had slit my tires.

Chapter 16

"Any idea who is mad enough at you to cut up your tires, sis?"

"Besides you and Neil?"

She made a face. "Ha, ha. At least I have an alibi. I was with you."

A tow truck had quickly moved my car to the garage and he went right to work switching out the old tires.

"A disgruntled student?"

Cindy laughed and shook her head. "Even your suckiest classes don't warrant four slashed tires."

"I have sucky classes?"

She gently put an arm around me. "Of course not. If it's not a student or an ex-lover," she paused and looked at me expectantly. I shook my head. "Then I'm guessing someone has heard that you are poking around in Jerry's murder, and they're not happy about it."

"Then they would be happy to know that I don't know anything."

"Know anything about what, Mariah?" A familiar voice checked in behind me.

I turned around. "Nothing, Maya. I know nothing about anything, except maybe yoga."

The reporter smiled and pointed her camera toward my car up on the racks. "Want to tell me what happened?"

"Nope."

Maya lowered her camera and turned toward me. "I'll find out anyway."

I stepped toward her and got in her face. This woman was really starting to irritate me. "How is it that whenever anything bad happens, you're right there, Maya? Hmm, why it that?"

Maya laughed and made a face. "I have a police scanner, Mariah. I hear everything that goes on."

I stepped back. She had a point.

She waved at my car. "So, nothing? You're not going to give me anything?"

"Time to move on, Anderson." Cindy spoke up from the corner of the garage, where she was watching both the mechanic and Maya.

"Thanks anyway, Sheriff." Maya waved and scooted out of the garage.

"Stupid reporter." I was still muttering when Cindy came and stood by my side.

"Interesting, though." Cindy caught my eye. "I didn't call in your tire incident. It wasn't on the scanner."

We stared at each other and Cindy put up a hand as if telling me to "stop."

"I will follow up. You consider taking this as a sign that you should back off and focus on your budding yoga business. And just be grateful that Anderson was out of town last month when you were accused of murder."

I nodded reluctantly, but not because I agreed I should back off. She was right that I needed to focus on my business. I also needed to help Josie's family.

Throughout the rest of the evening and as I was crawling into bed, I mulled over our conversation and the sudden appearance of Maya Anderson. I couldn't figure out what her motive might be. What was her connection to Jerry McIntyre?

I tossed and turned under the covers as I thought about Tamara. Did I really believe that she had set up Angelica to take the fall for the murder she had committed? I hated the idea that someone so well known in the yoga community would do such a thing, but I had to face facts. Just because someone practiced the physical asanas of yoga did not mean they practiced the spiritual principles. I would have hoped, however, that someone who supposedly helped students become "goddess-like" would follow them.

The next morning after the early vinyasa class, I decided to see what Tamara was up to. Deangelo was still working on projects at his mother's house, leaving Tamara with nothing to do. Besides, I was pretty sure they were still on the outs.

Locking the studio behind me, I wandered toward the hotel, not sure what I would say if I ran into her. "Hi, Goddess Tamara, did you kill Jerry?" did not seem like it would go over well.

As I neared the hotel, Tamara stepped down the front steps and darted around the corner. I hurried to see what she was up to just in time to see her head toward her car.

Dang it! I broke into a run in the opposite direction. My car was parked in front of The Yoga Mat today so I could keep an eye on it. Besides, I wanted whoever slashed my tires to know I had survived their little taunt. I hopped into the car and revved the motor, then made a quick U-turn and headed back toward the hotel. I wasn't even sure if Tamara would still be in the vicinity, but I crossed my fingers and sent a silent prayer for *satya*.

As I reached the intersection, I looked both ways and glimpsed Tamara's little red convertible heading north of town. I bolted around the corner to follow her, slowing down as I got closer. I didn't want her to see it was me behind her, but in a small town like Jasper, there just wasn't a lot of traffic on the road. On the other hand, there weren't that many places for her to go either.

We followed the road northeast past the old high school. I still grimaced every time I passed the decrepit old building, ever since a killer had tried to take me down there last month. Falling through the wooden floors of the old place actually had saved my life and possibly Stormy's, too, who had gone out to the school to meet me.

I couldn't figure out where Tamara was going until she slowed near the turnoff for the trailhead at Jasper River. The red convertible turned in, but I kept going, just in case she was wise to me trailing her. I made another U-turn, then pulled my car into the trailhead parking lot, hoping I would see the convertible before Tamara saw me. A flash of red in the dirt-packed parking lot alerted me that Tamara had pulled in and parked.

I turned in the opposite direction, pulling my nondescript sedan into a spot behind some bushes. As Tamara walked toward the trailhead, I ducked down, my head practically on the passenger seat. When I lifted my head, Tamara was gone. I hopped out and walked toward the trailhead. Looked like we would be doing some hiking today.

The path was well-worn by years of high schoolers trekking to the river to party or make out. I shuddered. I hoped I didn't come across any half-dressed teen-agers. I might have to call their moms.

Every once in a while, I caught sight of Tamara, still striding purposefully down the trail. She was not just out for a gentle stroll. She was up to something. When she stopped abruptly at a fork in the path, I almost walked right out into the open. Instead, I dove into the bushes, scratching my arms, as I tried to get out of sight. I held my breath waiting to find out if she had seen me, but all I heard were footsteps walking lightly away.

I crept out from behind the tree, rubbing the blood spots away on my arm as I gingerly stepped back to the path. A flash of pink off to the left let me know she had gone that way, so I followed. We were getting close to the river, which meant we would run out of trail soon.

Just before the last bend, I slipped off the path and behind some large boulders. The river was just on the other side. As I started to peer around the rock to see what Tamara was up to, a hand reached around my face, covering my mouth and pulling me backwards.

The hand muffled my screams as I fought off my attacker.

"Stop, Mariah, stop! It's me!"

I fell backwards hard onto my butt with an "oof."

"CeCe, what are you doing here?"

She motioned for me to be quiet, then leaned in. "I followed Lou here. Apparently, there's a hook-up."

She pointed to the other side of the rocks while offering me a hand. I accepted, then limped over to the edge of the rocks. My mouth fell open as I peered around the side. Lou Alveretti of Luigi's Pizzeria approached from the right side. Tamara and Lou hugged, then sat down on a log by the river, their arms around each other and their heads leaned in close as they talked in low murmurs. Tamara gently touched his face and brushed his hair away. He smiled into her eyes.

"I totally did not see that coming." I turned to CeCe. "What does this mean?"

She shrugged. "It's not illegal to hook up with someone."

"Says the boss who hooked up with her barista."

She smiled and waved her hand to push aside my words, then took my hand to pull me away from the river and up the trail. We kept low to the path so they wouldn't see us leave.

When we had trekked partway back to the car, we stopped and sat on a stump to process what we had seen.

"Do you think they did it together?"

"Why would they do it?"

I crossed my ankle over my knee and set my elbow on top. "Maybe she did want revenge, if the rumors are accurate."

"First, we thought he did it because he was hooking up with Sandy. Now you think he did it because he is hooking up with Tamara, who is way too young for him, by the way."

"Again, you're dating your barista, who is twelve years younger than you."

CeCe made a face. "Yes, but Lou is like fifty and she's, what, twenty-eight, twenty-nine? That's nearly a generation. What can they possibly have in common?"

I frowned and slumped onto the stump. "What I want to know is this: Why is everyone in this town hooking up except me?"

She blew out her breath in disgust. "I wouldn't say everyone. Josie's not. She's married to her job. Besides, that sheriff's detective has tried to ask you out at least twice. You keep ditching him."

I tilted my head to look at her. "What are you talking about?"

"When he suggested you go to the Movie Night? And you said, 'sure, let's bring Stormy?'"

"What? No. No. Seriously, what?"

CeCe looked at me, her eyes twinkling, and laughed. She nudged me with her elbow. "Yeah, seriously, he was trying to ask you out."

"Was he upset?"

CeCe shrugged. "I didn't exactly talk to him about it. I just saw the signs."

"Anything else I've missed?"

"Just about every time he offers to walk you someplace."

I scoffed. "Don't be silly. I am perfectly capable of taking care of myself and getting myself to the studio and home and—" I put on my fake TV voice – "golly, Lassie, just about anywhere else I need to go."

CeCe dropped her head to her chest and stared at her feet as she kicked dirt clouds from her shoes, a completely useless activity since we still had more trail to hike.

"That's the problem, Mariah." Her voice was soft. "You act like you don't need anyone. So that makes it hard for a guy to ask you out." She shifted on the stump to look me in the eyes. "It's okay to let a man take care of you sometimes. It's kind of nice to have someone open the door, walk me home, even cook my dinner."

A lump filled my throat that I didn't expect. "I make it hard? I do that?" I looked away from her and leaned my shoulder into hers. "Wow, I do that, yes, I do that."

I clasped my hands over my arms. "I'm not sure how to change that. Since Lee and I split up and really even before we divorced, I got used to taking care of things on my own. I'm comfortable with myself, with not leaning on a man."

CeCe smiled and leaned back into me. "I know. It was hard for me, too. I'm proud to be a strong woman, but…" She sat up and stretched out her arms. "It's nice to have a good foot rub from time to time."

"He rubs your feet? You are so lucky."

CeCe stood up and held out her hand to me. "You could have it, too, Mariah. Just pay as much attention to the men in your life as you do to students in your class. By the way, I cannot believe you called me out like that in class the other day."

"What are you talking about?"

CeCe mimicked my voice. "Pause in Goddess. Open your mouth as wide as you can. And then exhale, closing your mouth. I knew you were talking about me. I could feel my face being all tense and grim."

"See." I nudged her with my elbow. "You didn't even need me to call you out. You're really listening to your own body. And you weren't the only one, by the way."

Just then we heard voices from the river and looked at each other. *Oh, crumb.* We'd talked too long and now we might get caught anyway. CeCe pushed me off the trail into some bushes, scratching up my other arm, as she dove the other way.

We had just stopped moving around when the voices got louder, then steps passed our hiding places on the path. Tamara and Lou talked softly as they wound their way back up the trail. I only hoped they wouldn't see my car sitting off the trailhead.

Once they were safely past, CeCe and I pushed ourselves up and brushed off the dirt and leaves. I held out my arms.

"At least I have a matching set." I spied the scratches ruefully.

"C'mon, let's get some disinfectant on them."

"Disinfectant? I don't think that's what you use on scratches. That's what you use on bathrooms."

CeCe just walked away, striding back up the path.

Chapter 17

CeCe and I met back at her coffee shop. A triple mocha with extra chocolate was in order. But I turned down the offer of a chocolate doughnut.

"No, thanks, I'm trying to cut down."

CeCe stared pointedly at my mocha.

"You're right. I'll take the doughnut, too."

We watched out her front picture window as Lou drove past in a pickup truck, turning at the end of the block, no doubt to park behind his store, just as I usually did at The Yoga Mat. That made me think. We parked in the same alleyway every day. It would have taken Lou no time at all to slash my tires last night and, of course, he had access to plenty of knives in his restaurant.

"Mariah? Did you hear what I said?"

I looked away from Luigi's to find CeCe standing over my table, the chocolate doughnut on a plate in her hand. "Sorry. What?"

"What are you thinking about?" She shoved the plate in front of me and sat down across from me, reaching over to cut off a piece of the doughnut.

"Does Lou ever come in? I don't remember ever seeing him in here." I licked whipped cream from the top of my mug.

CeCe shook her head. "He says he only drinks Italian coffee that he makes himself."

I looked at her in surprise. "Has he tried your cappuccinos? They are delish."

She bowed her head, placing one hand over her heart, in acknowledgement. "I learned from the pros. I've offered to make him one, but he says no. It's okay. Not everyone has to come into my shop."

I frowned. "We go to his restaurant all the time. It's only fair that he shops at our stores."

"Not everyone goes to your yoga studio."

"True. I don't expect all the other store owners to buy a six-month pass. But he could stop in for a cup of coffee sometimes. Would it kill him to reciprocate?"

"Probably not the best choice of words right now."

My eyes met CeCe's and widened. "Probably not."

The front door of Luigi's Pizzeria opened. Lou stepped out and propped open one side of the double doors. He looked up and down the street, waving to a few people he knew, motioning for them to come to the restaurant, a big smile across his face.

Impulsively, I jumped up and raced out CeCe's front door, hurrying across the street to Luigi's.

"Lou!" I waved as I jaywalked across Main Street.

He turned toward me, the smile fading from his face when he saw who it was. That's not exactly the most heartening sight.

"What can I do for you, Mariah?" His face was impassive. "I would think you're pretty well stocked up on pizza for a while."

I smiled as charmingly as I could. "You can't ever have too much pizza, Lou."

He didn't even crack a smile, just waited, one hand on the door.

"Lou, I need to talk to you for five minutes."

"About what?"

"Sandy and Tamara."

Lou froze, then he eyed me warily. "What about them?"

I moved closer to him. "They are both connected to Jerry. They both had reason to want him dead and now you're connected to him, too. Do you really want to go to jail for one of them?"

He backed away from me, concern flickering over his face. "Why would I go to jail for them?"

"For being an accessory to a murder?" That was the only thing I could think of that sounded remotely reasonable.

"Why would I kill Jerry?" He let go of the door and crossed his arms.

I motioned him to the bench along the sidewalk. "Five minutes. Please."

He followed me to the bench and sat down at one end, looking pointedly at his watch. "Five minutes. It's nearly lunch time and I have a business to run. I thought you did, too."

I glanced at my watch. He did have a point about that.

"You never answered our question before. Are you having an affair with Sandy?" It couldn't hurt to ask him again.

He hesitated, then shook his head. "Not anymore. Well, I don't know." He looked down the street toward the Corner Mercantile and leaned closer to me, lowering his voice. "We have been spending some time together. Adult time, if you know what I mean?"

Why did people say that? Of course, I knew what he meant. "Go on."

"Her marriage to Jerry was a sham. He was drunk all the time. Mostly, she just took care of him like a mother, keeping him out of trouble."

"Why didn't she divorce him?"

Lou's eyes darted from side to side. "I probably shouldn't say. It's not really my business but the store has belonged in his family for years. Her name was not on the title. He held that over her, told her she would be out on the streets if she divorced him. It was the only thing he had to keep her there. Even he knew he would fall apart without her."

"Wow. That's a tough life for her." I bit my lip and looked down the street. "Enough of a motive to kill her husband?"

Lou scoffed. "Why now? She's put up with him all these years. Why would she kill him now?"

I looked at him pointedly. "You, Lou." *Ugh. Why did that have to rhyme?* "You."

He veered away from me, nearly coming off his seat. "Me? You think she killed her husband to be with me?"

Horror flew across his face and landed there. He covered his mouth with his hand as he considered what I had said, finally, shaking his head and looking me straight in the eye, pressing his hands into his knees.

"I know she can come across as gruff, Mariah, but Sandy is a good woman. She works harder than anyone I know. She's generous. Did you know she has funded several scholarships at the community college?"

I didn't know that. I shook my head.

"I'm sure she didn't kill her husband." At that, his eyes flickered away from mine and he sat back on the bench, crossing his arms. His voice said he was sure, but his body didn't seem to be on board.

"If she is so wonderful, why have you been hooking up with the Goddess Tamara?"

I hadn't been sure I was going to ask the question but was glad I did. His response was classic: He choked on his own spit, coughing and taking a minute to catch his breath.

"Why would you think that?" he gasped out.

I cocked my head and looked at him. "Don't even try to deny it, Lou."

He hesitated, then smiled sheepishly. He held his hands in the air as if they held a gift. "Tamara," he said her name gently, "has this spark, this light about her. I feel drawn to her."

"Like a moth to a flame? That's not always a good thing."

He laughed. "I know it seems crazy. It's just been a few days, but I feel alive inside, like I'm twenty years younger again."

"Maybe because she is twenty years younger than you?"

"Now, Mariah, don't be bitter just because it's not you." Lou shook his head at me as if I were a naughty child.

"What? No! Ew, Lou." *Well, that was another unfortunate rhyme.*

I leaned away from him.

He wiped his hands together, then pressed them into his thighs as he stood up. "I enjoyed spending time with Sandy. I love Tamara. But I didn't kill Jerry, Mariah, and I don't know who did. Go bark up some other tree and leave me in peace."

"Uh, Lou, just one more thing. Why don't you ever go to the other local shops on Main Street, besides Corner Mercantile, for obvious reasons? We all eat at Luigi's Pizzeria, but you never reciprocate by coming into our places of business."

Lou seemed taken by surprise. He paused, one hand on the bench and looked down the street. "I go to the shops."

"Which ones?"

"I've been to the hardware store," he said, his chin lifted in plain defiance.

I shook my head. "C'mon, Lou. Be a team player. Someone besides me is going to notice and then perhaps we won't be eating quite as much pizza."

Lou's mouth fell open and then he started to laugh. "Are you threatening to boycott my restaurant if I don't do yoga at your studio? Are you kidding?"

He kept laughing as he waved to someone down the street and strolled back into his pizzeria.

I sat on the bench for a moment longer. *Jerk. Maybe I would boycott his pizzeria.*

I believed him about Jerry, though – mostly. He didn't seem like a killer to me, but then again, no one I had talked to seemed like a killer. I let my head fall back over the top edge of the bench. Maybe Neil was right. Maybe I shouldn't be investigating based on my gut instincts. What was it he always said? Follow the evidence. This particular evidence led me to a dead end.

I jumped up and walked back across the street to CeCe's. She met me at the door, ushering me back to my table. "Well?"

"He did have an affair with Sandy. He is having one with Tamara. I don't think he killed Jerry, but he laughed at me when I suggested he reciprocate with other businesses on Main Street, so I'm keeping him on the suspect list."

"He seems like a real prize," CeCe scoffed as she shifted her gaze to the front doors of Luigi's.

"Yeah, too bad he makes such good pizza."

Chapter 18

The next day, Stormy rode shot gun and gave directions out to the part of the river where they had dug up the Red Jasper. We'd closed the studio after the two o'clock class so we could both go. Josie sat in the back seat and pouted most of the way. I wasn't thrilled to be driving back out to the river. Twice in one week seemed a bit much, even though it didn't take long. Josie wasn't happy about it either.

"I just don't see what we're going to come up with at the river." Josie crossed her arms and slumped in the seat, looking out the window.

I glanced in the rear-view mirror. "We might come up with nothing or we might find a clue to clear your sister. Stay focused, Josie."

She made a face, then dipped her head in acknowledgement.

We reached an outcropping on the east side of the river and pulled off to the shoulder of the road. Stormy jumped out of the car, Josie slowly moving behind her, her reluctance telegraphing itself loud and clear.

I came up behind her and hooked my arm in hers. "It's all going to work out, Jos," I whispered. "Keep the faith."

Josie sighed and clutched my arm to her for a brief moment, then released me. We walked comfortably toward the river, Stormy skipping along ahead.

I smiled at her exuberance. She was a far different young woman than the one I had first met in my yoga class, wow, just over a month ago. The thing was, I wasn't sure who had changed the most – her or me?

Stormy guided us up the trail, turning toward the left rather than the more heavily marked right trail at a fork in the road. The air was cool between the trees and felt good on my skin.

Stormy waved toward the right-side trail, the Rivers Edge Trail. "Too many people are on that trail, so we always sneak off to the left."

We waved her on and followed up a slight grade, then down a longer downhill. After about a ten-minute easy walk, Stormy paused, looked around, then stepped off the trail into the bushes.

Josie and I stopped and looked at the trail ahead of us. The bushes seemed to have swallowed Stormy whole.

Her head popped out of the bushes and she turned toward us. "Are you guys coming or not?"

We scooted up the hill and slipped into the bushes behind her. The branches felt soft and damp, so close to the river. We could hear it flowing past, lapping against the banks. Stormy slowly walked along the banks, then stopped.

"We're not the only ones who have been here." Her face looked dismayed. "I wonder who told about our super-secret spot."

Josie shrugged as she leaned in close to look at the footprints. "At first glance, it looks like just one person. See," – she pointed to prints in the mud – "it's the same shoe, same size, same tread. Maybe someone just stumbled upon your 'super-secret spot.' It happens."

Stormy studied the riverbank, then drew us further downstream. She stopped and peered into the water, then took off her shoes and stepped into the river. Josie watched her with dismay.

"Stormy, as an officer of the law, I have to tell you to use caution and perhaps rethink stepping into the river at this time."

Stormy cracked a smile in Josie's direction. "Thank you for your concern, deputy, but it's not against the law, so I'm moving on."

"Fair enough."

I stepped to the very edge of the bank to get a better look. Stormy looked up quickly. "Mariah, be careful. Those banks give way with hardly any notice and then you'll end up swimming."

I stepped back from the edge but tried to see what Stormy was doing. She pulled a kitchen spoon out of her pocket and bent down toward the water.

"You have to be careful," she pointed out. "If you forget and sit your butt in the water, you look like you had an accident, if you know what I mean."

"We all know what you mean." Once Josie started muttering under her breath, I could tell she was growing irritated with Stormy.

"Aha!" Stormy held out her hand holding a small Red Jasper stone. Josie and I each took a turn holding it.

The stone looked like the one that was on the sidewalk by Jerry. I realized that neither stone had been polished like the ones in the Corner Mercantile.

"So, how much could you sell this for?" Josie wanted to know.

Stormy shrugged. "We used to sell them to Sandy for a dollar a pop, but then she decided to dig them herself. I think she followed us out here one day and found our spot." Realization dawned on her face. "That's probably whose footprints we saw."

I frowned. "At her age? I mean, she's not old, but she seems old enough to not want to go traipsing around the riverbank."

"She was our main business, so when she bailed, we quit digging up Red Jasper. It just wasn't worth our time anymore."

I began to wonder if I could dig up Red Jasper, too, just to use in the studio or at home. I inched my way down the riverbank, holding on to tree branches so I could peer over the side into the water.

"How do you know you're in a good spot?" I had to raise my voice for Stormy to hear me over the fast-moving water.

"Just look for a flash of red and start digging." Stormy looked up toward me, miming digging with a small shovel.

I crept downriver a little further, then, getting on my hands and knees to keep my center of gravity lower, I leaned my head out over the bank and grinned. There! A bit of red shined through the water.

I reached down and had just grasped my hand around the rock when I felt a shove on my backside. I held tight to the stone as I screamed and tumbled into the river.

"Mariah!"

Chapter 19

Josie and Stormy ran along the riverbank to find me struggling to turn onto my backside in the shallow river, clinging to a tree branch that had swung out over the water.

"Hang on, Mariah!" Josie turned away from me and returned with a large stick in one hand. She stepped to the edge of the shore, then looped her arm through Stormy's, who had wrapped her arms around a small tree to anchor herself.

Josie handed the branch to me. I reached for it, tightening my abdomen so I would not be dead weight during the rescue. I was able to lift myself out of the water and finally put my feet down.

"Don't stand up!" Josie barked at me to keep my center of gravity low and walk slowly toward her, hanging onto the stick. "Check before you step each foot down that you're not stepping in between the rocks."

I concentrated on hanging on to the stick as the current rushed past as I crept carefully toward the shore. When I finally reached the bank, Stormy and Josie reached out to grab each of my shoulders and dragged me onto the bank and then into dirt and bushes.

"Ouch! Thanks, girls. Stop – ouch! – dragging me now!" I wasn't sure which hurt more – being pulled by my shoulders or dragged through the dirt. It felt like a toss-up.

They let loose of me, letting me fall onto the bank. Putting my hands beneath my shoulders – just the way I tell my yoga students – I pushed up and away into a kneeling position to catch my breath before standing.

"Mariah, I told you the riverbank gives way easily. What were you thinking?"

"I wasn't thinking anything. Someone pushed me into the river!"

Josie shook her head. "There was no one there but you, Mariah. It doesn't make sense."

I held up my hand as if I could stop her words. "All I know is that hands were suddenly on my backside and pushing me into the river."

"Did you see who it was?"

I shook my head and peered at the two of them. "It happened too fast. For all I know, it could have been one of you."

Stormy gasped. Josie made a face.

"Stay here," Josie ordered. She reached behind her back and unhooked her gun, then started creeping through the woods away from the river. She paused beside a tree stand, one hand on a tree as she slowly looked around. Her eyes darting back and forth, she pulled her cell phone from her pocket and pointed it toward the ground. Stepping gingerly around something, she took a few more pictures, then tucked her cell phone away.

She walked, her head down, across the trail and into the bushes near where Mariah had been standing.

"I think you're right, Mariah. It looks like someone was standing over here." She pointed to the tree stand. "Then they crossed the trail here." She pointed to the bushes. "See, and we wouldn't have been able to see them from this angle when they pushed you in."

She looked at me with a pointed expression. "I can't even imagine who you have managed to piss off. Again." She thought about it for a moment, staring off into the distance. Stormy kept rubbing my back.

"Did you tell anyone we were going to the river?" Josie finally asked.

I shook my head, then reconsidered. "Wait a minute. I did tell Sandy I might go dig up some Jasper, but I didn't say when. Maya Anderson might have overheard me, too. I have to say May sure seems to be everywhere I don't want her to be lately."

Josie stared at the ground in thought. "I don't know. That seems iffy."

"Um, Josie?"

Something in Stormy's tone prompted us both to turn and look at her.

"I might have said something to CeCe at the diner this afternoon." She stopped rubbing my back and clutched her arms around her waist, looking forlornly at Josie.

"At the diner? Where everyone and their brother could hear?" Josie's tone was incredulous.

"Now, Josie, how could she have known this would happen?" I jumped in to back up Stormy. "It's not like it was a big secret anyway. Cindy probably already knows we're here."

Josie couldn't help it. She cracked a smile, then laughed out loud. "You're right. That woman has eyes everywhere."

We all laughed together, Stormy looking much relieved.

"Stormy, do you remember who was there when you talked to CeCe?"

Stormy closed her eyes and nodded slowly. "Sure, let's see, there was that lady from the pet store and her weird clerk, Mr. Sampson from the insurance place—"

I had to interrupt. "Stormy, anyone who might have wanted to hurt me? Anyone connected with Jerry McIntyre's death, for instance?"

Her eyes flew open. "Oh, definitely. Maya, Jennifer from Safety Blanket, um, Sandy, Tamara and Lou. Oh, yeah, Sandy came in and saw Tamara and Lou. She looked mad." Then she shrugged. "That's all I can remember."

"Wait! Did you say Lou from Luigi's was at CeCe's shop?" I grabbed Stormy by the arm, not believing what I'd heard.

Stormy tried to back away from me. "Yeessss."

"He's never stepped foot in there before. I got on his case about it the other day, about how he never frequents the other shops on Main Street." I was mentally patting myself on the back. Lou had changed his tune. Nice job, even if I do say so myself.

Then I blew out my cheeks as my heart sank. "However, that's pretty much all of our suspects in one room. That's not so helpful."

Josie took me by the arm. "Maybe, maybe not. We just don't know yet if it's useful."

Even as I smiled weakly, I started to shiver and I ached all over. Josie noticed. "Let's go, Mariah. We'll find somewhere to get you warmed up."

Josie drove the car back to my house, a mostly silent ride, dropping Stormy at her apartment on the way. When we got to my house, Josie stopped in the driveway and turned to me. She tilted her head thoughtfully as if she was just about to say something when her cell phone buzzed.

She listened a few moments, a half-smile breaking out on her face. When she clicked off, she turned her body back toward mine.

"Good news: They've released Angelica. She is at home with Mama and the boys already!"

"Josie, that's awesome. Did they find the real killer?"

Josie paused, playing with her phone, then looked back up at me, her face tight with worry. "That's the bad news. They've arrested Tamara and Deangelo."

Chapter 20

"First Angelica, then Tamara and Deangelo? Who's next on the list of least-likely suspects – me?" I stopped myself and looked at Josie. "Never mind. I don't even want to go down that path."

"Good choice."

I sat back on the passenger seat for a moment and wondered what the best plan of action was. I shivered again.

"Okay, first I'm going to dry off and put on fresh clothes, then we can drive into town. Do you mind waiting a few minutes?"

"Nope." Josie unclicked the seat belt, exited the car and followed me into the house. The banging of cabinets and pans echoed from downstairs while I jumped into a hot shower. At first, the water was so hot it hurt my frozen skin. Then it began to tingle until finally I just felt warm again. I signed in contentment. Another pan banged, reminding me to hurry up.

I dried off and dressed quickly in another pair of yoga clothes. That was definitely one of the advantages to being a yoga instructor and studio owner. No one looked twice at me for wearing workout gear at all hours of the day. Truth be told, I had very few clothes that weren't yoga gear, particularly with the new brands of yoga clothes that bragged that you could wear them to the office.

I hurried downstairs to find Josie sitting at my kitchen table with a cup of tea and a bowl of soup before her. She waved me to the other chair and brought over another bowl of soup and a cup of tea.

"Thank goodness you keep canned soup on hand."

"Usually I make it from scratch, but the canned stuff is helpful in a pinch." I daintily sipped from my soup spoon, knowing that Josie was casting an evil eye on me. Then I smiled. "Not really."

"I knew it." She leaned forward and sipped some of the soup from her bowl. "Still, it sure works when you're cold."

We quickly finished the soup, then hurried back to town, me to teach a class and Josie to track down Angelica and see if she could give her more information about Tamara.

Stepping into the studio, I spread out my mat at the front of the room and sat down, mindfully doing some pelvic rotations as I pondered the best poses to do in light of Tamara's arrest. I didn't know yet if she would still be available to teach on Saturday.

I decided a grounding sequence would help me and my students accept whatever was going to happen, so after warming up, I moved through a Dancing Warrior sequence, flowing from one Warrior to another in tune with the breath. I stepped into a Goddess pose, then moved into Malasana, a sort of yoga squat with my hands at my heart and my elbows pressing out my knees.

I paused in Malasana, letting my shoulders relax and pressing my forehead to my hands as if in prayer. What would happen now that Tamara was arrested? I didn't believe she killed Jerry, but did I know for sure? And could I completely discount what Jerry had said with his last breaths – "Goddess"?

Two classes later, I locked the studio doors, knowing what I had to do. I drove directly toward the Sheriff's Post. Josie was behind the front window when I came in.

She smiled the best Deputy-With-a-Desk-Job smile she could, then motioned me around to the side door. "Good news. They let Deangelo go. Apparently, he wasn't really under arrest in the first place."

I sighed in relief. "What happened?"

"He has an alibi. Surveillance video shows him at the hardware store right before he picked up Tamara that night. He was there for at least a half hour before he went to the hotel."

"He sure has spent a lot of time at the hardware store."

Josie shrugged. "Mama has a lot of projects."

"Why are you still on desk duty then?"

Josie glanced back over her shoulder to make sure no one was listening in. She leaned closer. "Angelica is not completely off the hook. She's wearing an ankle bracelet and is on house arrest for now."

Then she peered at me closer. "Why are you here?"

"I want to see Tamara."

Josie nodded and motioned me back to the front desk. She picked up the phone. A few moments later, Neil emerged from a side door and came into the lobby. At first he smiled, then his demeanor changed as he took me by the elbow to a lobby chair.

"What are you doing here, Mariah?"

"I came to see Tamara."

"She's in a jail cell waiting to make a plea in her case."

"She didn't do it."

"You don't know that." Neil's eyes were sad. I knew that in all his years in law enforcement, he had seen and encountered so many horrific scenes. "The evidence points to her."

I crossed my arms and leaned away from Neil, deciding to try another tack. "I want to see her. She is supposed to present a workshop at my studio this weekend, and if I have to cancel it, I will lose a ton of money. Plus, my reputation will be compromised because my workshops will be deemed unreliable."

My eyes challenged him to fight me on this request, knowing what it could do to my business, which was just recovering from last month's murder.

Neil crossed his arms in response, He looked at me a long time, then he nodded. "Deemed unreliable, eh? Okay, you can talk to her.

But if she tells you anything important, I need to know about it, Mariah."

"Thank you." I made no concession about telling him what I learned. Maybe I would, maybe I wouldn't.

I followed the guard down the narrow hall I had walked with Josie just the day before. Truth be told, I had spent more than my fair share of time in the Jasper Sheriff's Department holding cells. I might have to rethink these "investigations."

Tamara was sitting in a cell, her back against the wall, eyes closed. She opened them when I came through the door. Sadness practically spilled from them. The guard wouldn't open the cell to let me in, so I sat down on the concrete floor just outside the cell and leaned forward against the bars. I wanted her to know that I was with her, that I believed in her.

"What can I do to help?" I asked softly.

Tamara closed her eyes again and shook her head. "I just feel so defeated, Mariah. I don't know why I'm here. I didn't kill anybody or ask anyone else to kill anybody."

"I know."

"You do?" She sat up, looking surprised. "What do you mean?"

I shrugged. "I don't think you're a killer. I don't think you're a very good girlfriend for Deangelo, but I don't think you're a killer."

Tamara laughed shortly. She swung her legs over the edge of the bed and moved down to the floor, her back resting against the bed.

I looked around the cell. "I had a stay in here, you know. They thought I killed someone, too, so I know what you're going through. For what it's worth, I figured the less I moved, the fewer germs I was liable to touch."

She looked around the cell and agreed. "I can't figure out where to sit without touching something."

"Tamara, tell me why they arrested you. Why does Neil think you killed Jerry McIntyre?"

Tamara's shoulders together and she seemed to briefly fold in on herself. She looked around the room, then crept over beside me just on the other side of the bars.

"We – my family – used to visit Jasper when I was a kid. My dad loved the outdoors here and Mom just liked the peace and quiet. Dad had an old aunt that lived here for a while, so we stayed with her."

I nodded silently.

Tamara tightly clasped her hands together. "Sometimes I would go to the Corner Mercantile and Sandy and Jerry let me help out, stock shelves and stuff like that to earn pocket money while we were here. They seemed really sweet. At first."

Tamara realized her hands were clasped and released them, alternately stretching them out and fisting them as her brow furrowed.

"Then one summer, when I was alone in the storeroom with Jerry, he-" Tamara looked away. "He attacked me and molested me. If Sandy hadn't come into the storeroom, I don't know what would have happened. She saw what was going on and took me out of the room, helped me straighten my clothes. She calmed me down and gave me some soda and then sent me home. Before I left the store, she took my face in her hands and said that if I told anyone, she would deny it."

We sat silently. I grieved the sadness of the young Tamara.

"We never went back to Jasper."

"Did you tell your parents?"

"Not until we went home a few days later. My parents were furious, but I told them no one else would believe me. I begged them not to say anything. It would be my word against Sandy's."

"I heard Sandy and Jerry paid your parents a lot of money to keep them quiet."

Tamara scoffed.

"So Neil thinks you stabbed Jerry in retaliation?"

Tamara laughed shortly. "As if." She turned to look me square in the face. "I forgave Jerry and Sandy long ago. I talk in my workshop about a traumatic event that I learned to put behind me. I love that little girl who didn't know how to stand up for herself."

I smiled at her. "Because she grew up and learned to stand on her own two feet."

Tamara's eyes sparkled. "It's part of my story, but it's not my whole story. Yoga and meditation were so important in getting me here." She paused and looked around us. "Well, not *here* specifically, but you know what I mean."

I did know. Yoga had taken me to a new life, too.

"Did you know Jerry had a flyer for your workshop in his hand?" I wanted to ask her about that, but I didn't know yet if I would mention that Jerry had said "Goddess."

Tamara tilted her head to the side in puzzlement. "Why would he care? It's been fifteen years and, if I've heard correctly, he's been drunk for most of that time?"

I couldn't answer that question any more than she could.

We sat in silence for a few moments longer, then she looked at me again. "So why don't you think I'm a good girlfriend for Deangelo?"

"Lou at Luigi's Pizza."

Silence greeted my statement. She looked over, a little sheepishly. "How do you know about that?"

I waved a hand. "That's not important. I just know. When did you hook up with him?"

"Right after I got to town." A soft smile appeared on her face and her cheeks flushed. "We just connected, right? It was intense right from the start." She frowned. "I do feel kind of bad about Deangelo, though. He's a good guy."

"Does he know about you and Lou?"

"He probably does now. We did go into the coffee shop together today."

A light bulb came on. "Wait a minute. You're the one who made Lou go to CeCe's?"

Tamara nodded. "After he told me what you had said about him not going to the other businesses, I told him karma would bite him in the butt if he didn't change his behavior. So we went to CeCe's. Their lemon jasmine tea is amazing, right?"

I had to give her that one. She was correct about CeCe's tea. "One more question, Tamara. Did you ever hear of any other girls who might have been assaulted by Jerry?"

She thought for a moment. "Only one other that I knew of. Angelica."

The air whooshed out of my lungs. Angelica had been attacked by Jerry, too? Did Neil and Cindy know?

The guard cleared his throat and tapped his wrist to tell me my time was almost up. I gave him the "just a minute" sign and clambered to my feet.

"Do you think they will let you out before Saturday?"

Tamara shrugged. "Maybe you should cancel the workshop?"

"Let's wait a day or two and see what shakes out."

CeCe and I would be poking around and something was bound to turn up.

Tamara blew me a kiss. "At least this is giving me a chance to practice *satya*. I can't be anything but who I am here, right?"

Chapter 21

Neil sat in the lobby of the Sheriff's Post, his feet stretched out in front of him and his arms crossed behind his head. I should have known he would still be waiting for me. He appeared deep in thought, but his eyes flickered to mine as the door clicked open and Josie gestured for me to walk through.

She quickly closed the door behind me and within a few moments was back at her post at the front desk, her eyes on the papers in front of her instead of at Neil or me, but I was pretty sure she wouldn't miss a thing.

Neil turned his head to look at me, pulling in his legs and patting the seat beside him. I remained standing, my legs still too shaky after what Tamara had just told me.

"Are you okay, Mariah?"

I quickly glanced at Josie, then sat down. "We need to talk."

He hopped up from his seat, pulling me with him. "Let's walk."

Neil motioned to Josie he was leaving. She nodded at him and made a note, then raised her eyebrows at me as soon as he looked away. We turned away from Main Street, taking us down the sidewalk away from downtown. We walked for a few moments in silence, he with his hands in his pockets.

Finally he spoke.

"What's going on?"

"Tamara just told me that Angelica was assaulted by Jerry, too," I blurted out. "This could change everything! I might have been wrong about Angelina."

Neil stopped and put both hands on my shoulders. "Mariah, calm down. I know. Angelica told us. It was an attempted assault. Apparently, Jerry was too drunk most of the time to follow through."

I made a face. "But that doesn't change that he kept trying. I wonder if there are others?"

"Probably. It's been my experience that people like that don't just try once or twice. Is that what you went to see Tamara about?"

"No, it just came up."

We turned and started walking again, passing a few homes on the edge of town.

"You know why I was there. Why did you even ask that question?"

"It's an investigative technique. Always better to ask than assume. For instance, what were you doing at the river today?"

My mouth dropped open and I looked at my watch, then looked up admiringly. "Wow, you are good. We haven't even been back three hours yet. Sheriff Cindy is rubbing off on you."

He brushed off pretend lint from his shoulder.

He walked silently next to me. "What else did you learn?"

I shrugged. "I don't know, not being a trained investigator and all, I can't imagine that I would learn more than a big, strong deputy like you."

He stopped again to look at me, then grinned. "Flattery will get you nowhere, ma'am."

"Did you just call me 'ma'am'? And I was being sarcastic."

He tried to keep a straight face as he turned to walk some more. "I know. So you haven't learned anything else?"

I hurried to catch up. "I didn't say that. I've learned plenty. I'm just not sure how it all fits together."

"It's always a puzzle." He used his hands to demonstrate how things fit together. "Eventually one piece will fall into place, then another and another until suddenly you see how the whole thing fits together. At least, that's what they taught us in big, strong deputy investigator school."

Even from his peripheral vision, I could see the twinkle in his eye.

We stopped in our tracks. The sidewalk had run out. Turning around, we headed back toward the post.

"*Satya*," I whispered. "Finding the absolute truth."

"It's what I strive for every day." Neil shoved his hands back into his pockets as he walked. We walked in silence back to the post, pausing at the door.

"You're not going to quit looking into this, are you?" Neil paused with his hand on the door.

I shook my head. "I promised I would help."

Neil took a deep breath in response. "Let me know what you find out."

"I will if you will."

"No way."

"Okay, then, have a great day."

"*Okay then, have a great day.*"

My eyes widened in surprise. "Did you just mock me, detective?"

His eyes twinkled again. "Have a good day, Ms. Stevens."

With that, he opened the door and stepped inside.

Chapter 22

The morning Sun Salutations class was oddly full. I think Tamara's workshop had put yoga front and center in many students' minds, so they were coming to class more in preparation for Saturday. I sent her a silent "thank you" as I settled on my mat to open class.

Even Deangelo, Josie and Angelica turned up. Josie made a face as she caught my eye when they trooped through the door.

"You're spending an awful lot of time lately on your yoga practice, Josie," I commented from the safety of my office door.

Deangelo and Angelica grinned. "We dragged her with us," Angelica laughed, throwing an arm around her big sister.

Josie just shrugged. "It's not that I don't like yoga. It's starting to grow on me." With that, she grinned and took her mat to find a place in the studio.

Angelica lifted her leg to show me the bulky ankle bracelet she was wearing.

"Oh, no, they're really making you wear that thing?"

Angelica laughed. "Don't worry about it, Mariah. It's better than being in the jail cell. Apparently, they didn't want Tamara and me in there at the same time." She leaned in conspiratorially and lowered her voice. "Josie doesn't want me to talk about it. I guess they didn't want Tamara and me getting our story straight."

We moved quickly though the warmups and into the Sun Salutations flow. The other students didn't seem to notice Angelica's ankle gear, and it didn't get in her way much. She just worked around it, a small smile playing on her beautiful face.

Partway through, the front glass door swooshed open. I glanced to the side to see Neil standing in the lobby. He wasn't dressed for class, so I was pretty sure this wasn't a social call.

I kept my attention on my class. Neil knew the schedule. If he thought he would interrupt my class, he was sadly mistaken.

Once I had guided my students into a well-deserved *savasana*, that meditation time at the end of class, I padded over to the lobby with raised eyebrows. I leaned in close to him. "Can I help you, detective?"

Neil leaned toward my ear and whispered back. "I have some questions about the case, but I will wait until class is over. I just didn't want to miss you before you sprinted to the coffee shop."

I nodded and pulled away, my brows knit over my eyes. Was my schedule so well known? Did everyone in town know I raced to CeCe's after Sun Salutations? I couldn't eat much before class or I'd feel nauseous partway through – an uncomfortable experience had taught me that. So I was typically starving right after class.

I settled back on my mat, bell in hand, ready to bring the class out of meditation. Patricia's death in my class last month was still raw enough that I could feel myself tense up a little at this time every class. Would everyone sit up like they were supposed to?

Of course, they did. Patricia's death was an anomaly. I would need to let it go at some point.

As class ended and students began to exit the studio, I turned my attention back to Neil.

"What can I do for you, detective?"

"Detective?" Neil's eyes looked over my head. He nodded. "Good morning, Josie, Deangelo, Angelica."

The trio just looked at him, then continued gathering their gear.

"Well, this is awkward." Angelica let out a giggle.

Deangelo glared at Neil. Josie cleared her throat, then looked away.

Although I had misgivings about letting him out of an awkward situation, I wanted to spare Josie any more problems.

I touched Neil's arm and gestured toward my office. "I'll be right there."

He glanced sadly at the trio, then nodded, stepping silently toward my desk, where he propped himself on the edge. I noticed he could still see the front door.

"I'm sorry." I mouthed the words to the trio in the front lobby.

Josie shook her head and spoke softly. "It's not your fault. Just one of the perks of living in a small town."

"Truth, sistah." Angelica jumped up with a smile on her face. "Just one more reason to stay in L.A."

Josie swatted her, then they all reached for their gear, tossing their yoga mat carriers over their shoulders. They each gave me a hug as they passed by.

I turned back to Neil. "What's up, buttercup?"

He didn't crack a smile. "I want more information about your tires getting slashed. You want to tell me about it for the report?"

"Didn't Cindy file one?"

"That was the petty crime report. I want to know how it impacts my investigation into Jerry's murder."

Neil perched on the edge of my desk as I moved around to the chair behind it.

"I don't know that it does, Neil. I don't know what to think."

"Did you discuss the case with anyone besides your little group of co-conspirators?"

Pursing my lips, I shook my head.

"Did you overhear anyone talking about the case?"

Another head shake.

Neil tucked his notebook back into his jacket pocket and looked at me solemnly. "Mariah, just be careful. I have a very bad feeling about where this is going."

With that, Neil stood and strode out of the studio.

I leaned back in my chair, mulling over what he had said, my hands playing with a couple of Red Jasper stones from my desk. I opened my hand wide to look at them. "C'mon, Red Jasper. You're supposed to help bring justice into the world, right? Right? How about a little *satya* here?"

Rolling my eyes at myself, I sat back up, letting the stones fall to the desk. This is what I'd become during this investigation: I was talking to a couple of rocks. Literally. All I could do was laugh at myself, then my eyes focused on the two rocks. One was shiny and sparkly. This was one I had bought from the Corner Mercantile a while back.

The other one was dirty and dull. It was the one I had pulled from the river. Where had I seen some like it recently? Besides at Jerry's murder scene, I mean.

I toyed with them on my desk, feeling like I was missing something. Finally, I had to just set the thoughts aside. Perhaps it would come to me while I was teaching. The door flew open and a student stuck in her head.

"Hi, Mariah. Ready for my private?"

My stomach rumbled. *Dang it.* I had spent so long thinking about rocks and suspects that I forgot to run to CeCe's for breakfast.

The door flew open again. CeCe bolted in, both hands full. She shoved a cup and a bag at me. "Double-shot mocha with almond milk and a chocolate croissant."

My mouth fell open. My student watched from the lobby as she sat down to take off her shoes. I waved her into the studio. "I'll be right there."

"Take your time. That looks much more appetizing." She chuckled and pushed through the saloon doors into the studio.

"How did you know? Are you psychic now along with everything else?" I pulled the lid off the cup and drank deeply.

"Yes, I'm psychic, Mariah. I thought you knew that about me." CeCe just shook her head as I greedily bit into the croissant, moaning with delight. "That, and Josie told me Neil was waiting for you after class. I happened to see him walk past the shop, so I knew you were still here and I figured you could use a pick-me-up."

She leaned against the desk that Neil had recently vacated. "What did he want?"

"He wanted to know about the slashed tires and warn me off of investigating."

"Well, that was a complete waste of his time."

"Right? The thing is, CeCe, I feel like I'm close, but I just can't get my head around it."

She smiled and checked her watch. "Let it percolate – see what I did there? – and it will probably click at some point. I have to get back."

"Ha, ha." I hugged her and thanked her for the breakfast treats. After a couple of bites, I wrapped the leftovers in the napkin, wiped my mouth and pushed into the studio.

The rest of the day flew by. Cindy got tied up, so I took over her evening restorative yoga class. I don't know about the students, but I felt so relaxed at the end, I wanted to call a car to come drive me home.

The students wandered out of the studio, leaving me to quickly clean up and close the books for the night.

Yawning, I stepped out the front doors and locked them behind me. There was just one more stop to make before I headed for home. Saturday night was the monthly Movie Night, this month scheduled right after Tamara's workshop. That only gave me a couple of days to get her out of jail. I decided to finish my Silent Auction basket so I wouldn't have to think about it while I focused on springing Tamara.

I paused at the door of the Corner Mercantile. But what if Tamara really was guilty? What if, as Josie claimed, her yoga goddess persona was just an act and she really was capable of killing someone?

Clearly, my "locate the killer" radar was broken, if it had ever worked, for that matter.

"Hey, Mariah." Sandy stood at the front counter, wiping out some glasses that had apparently been on display a tad too long. "Don't usually see you out and about this late."

I glanced around the Corner Mercantile. I hadn't realized until she spoke that we were alone. I offered a rueful smile, acknowledging what she said. I tended to be home ready for bed at this time of night. "That's true. Just needed a couple of last-minute things for Movie Night."

"That danged Movie Night. I appreciate the business, but it's irritating to have to go to that thing every month."

I smiled as my eyes scanned the aisle. "I enjoy it. I like getting out and seeing everyone. Of course, I'm new in town, so that probably makes a difference."

As I reached for hand sanitizer on the bottom shelf, my eyes flicked to the back of the store, and my hand froze. Boxes stacked one on top of the other blocked the view of the back door. I sucked in a breath as I finished grabbing a bottle and putting it in my basket.

I stood up and swallowed hard. I couldn't see the back door. And if I couldn't see the back door, neither could Sandy's clerk. She had no alibi.

A sudden movement to my right made me jump.

"Did you find everything you needed, Mariah?" Sandy stood between me and the back door.

I laughed and nodded, shaking myself a little. "I guess I started daydreaming there for a minute."

"In the cleaning aisle? You need to improve your daydreams."

Sandy gave a little chin nod toward the counter and I headed toward it.

I stood awkwardly in front of the cashier's counter, then reached into my pocket and set a Red Jasper stone on the counter.

She stared at the rock, then her eyes flicked up to me, her face closely guarded. "What's this? Did you want to sell it? You know I don't buy Jasper anymore, Mariah. I dig it myself."

I played with the stone in my hand. "Right. At the river. You pushed me in."

Sandy scoffed. "Don't be silly. You were nowhere near where I dig."

"How do you know where we were?" I reluctantly lifted my eyes to meet hers. "I mean, if you weren't there, how do you know where we were?"

Sandy's gaze faltered briefly, then hardened again. "Small-town gossip, Mariah. That's all."

Part of my brain screamed at me to get out of the store, but another part urged me to get as much information as I could for Neil.

"When Jerry was stabbed, a rock fell from the killer's pocket and landed in Jerry's collar. Not just any rock. Red Jasper. Just like the ones you keep in your apron pocket there."

Sandy leaned her body away from the rock on the counter, automatically reaching up to touch the rocks in her smock apron. She literally looked down her nose at me. Then she shrugged and picked up her rag again, starting to wipe out of the glass in her hand. She gave a small smile.

"Sweet little Mariah playing detective again. Just because it turned out okay for you last time doesn't mean you're a detective. Maybe you should stick to yoga and leave detecting to the professionals."

Maybe you should stick to not killing people. Anger welled up inside, but I calmed myself with a breath. Anger would not help this particular situation.

I looked her directly in the eyes. "What if I told you the sheriff's department found a fingerprint on the Red Jasper rock at the crime scene?"

Sandy sized me up for a moment, probably trying to see if I was bluffing or not. I was, but I hoped she couldn't tell. It's not like she knew me that well, after all.

"I'd say you were lying." She finally spoke, swishing the rag around the glass. "I'd say the Sheriff's Department already has my husband's killer in jail."

She placed the glass that she'd been cleaning for the past few minutes back on the shelf with the rest, then calmly picked up the next one. She held it up to the light, squinting at it. Then she turned to face me, her hand in the glass and both hands on the counter. "And I'd wonder why you're trying to stir up trouble. Why can't you let it be?"

"Because an innocent woman is in jail."

Sandy spat in response. "That cow? If there's anything she is, it isn't innocent. She ruined Jerry's life. He was a good man, until she came to town and started spreading rumors."

Sandy suddenly banged the glass on the counter, startling me. "Who does she think she is, Miss High and Mighty, coming back to town, calling herself the 'goddess'? She was never Jerry's goddess."

Anger seeped from every part of Sandy's being. The realization of what she had just said hit me like a busload of bricks.

"She wasn't the goddess. You are." My eyes met hers. "*You're* the goddess. He loved you."

Sandy swallowed hard, her eyes finally dropping to her hands.

"It wasn't Tamara at all." It wasn't a question.

Sandy slowly nodded, her eyes on her hands as they tapped nervously on the counter.

"Do you want to talk about it?"

She shook her head, then shrugged her shoulders. "Doesn't matter now anyhow." She lifted her head and looked off as if the scene was replaying itself on the wall behind me, which, frankly, in her mind, it probably was.

"I was in the back picking up another box of stock, when he stumbled out the side door. I followed him outside and asked him where he thought he was going. He was probably still drunk from the night before. He never really sobered up anymore."

She stopped and wiped her nose on her long-sleeved T-shirt. I leaned forward and placed my hand on her arm to steady her. "He said he had to make amends to her, that he had hurt her and me both and the only way he knew to set it right was to tell her how wrong he had been and then turn himself in to the sheriff."

"I begged him to stop, to let us talk it out first. He was going to destroy everything we – *I* – had worked for the past 20 years. He had no right." Sandy's head dropped. "I was so angry, at first I didn't know what to do. I just went back inside to finish stocking. But that just made me look around at my beautiful store, that I've worked so hard to build up. I took the shortcut through the alley to the hotel. He was already at the top of the stairs when I grabbed his arm. He tried to shake me off, but he's been so far gone that he had no muscle anymore." She gave a small laugh. "I still had the knife I was using to open the boxes in my hand and I just stabbed him. He fell to the ground and hit his head."

"I'll never forget the sound of his head hitting that concrete as long as I live. Like an overripe pumpkin getting smashed." Tears appeared in the corners of her eyes but didn't fall over.

"Then I ran back to the store. My good-for-nothing clerk didn't even know I'd been gone. He probably didn't even take the buds out of his ears the whole time."

"Were you really going to let Tamara take the blame for his death?"

Sandy's eyes flashed. "My husband was never the same after that summer. She turned him into something he was not. He kept doing it and he never forgave himself."

"You never forgave him either."

Her lips became a single dry line. "He ruined his life *and* mine. How could I forgive either of them?"

Another realization hit home. My lips felt dried out. "And then Tamara came to town and hooked up with Lou, the pizza guy. That must have been a kick in the gut."

Sandy briefly closed her eyes and then exhaled. "I finally found someone who cared about me just for me. The fact that she showed up again to destroy something of mine … I hated her so much."

"Enough to let her go to prison for a crime you committed."

Sandy looked up triumphantly. "And she still will."

She stepped to the side of the counter, then slammed the glass on the counter, using her gloved hand to pick up the base, which still had a shard attached.

"Sandy! What are you doing?"

"I've got nothing left to lose, Mariah." She lunged toward me, catching me by surprise as she hit me low, causing me to step backwards, then tumble onto my backside over boxes stacked in the aisle.

She leapt toward me faster than I would have expected, so I rolled to my side to get away, which almost worked until she caught my foot and slashed my thigh with the glass shard in her hand.

I screamed in pain. Then I slammed my other foot into the side of her head, which made her loosen her hold on my foot so I kicked her hard with that one, too.

I scrambled away on my hands and knees, climbing quickly to my feet and heading toward the door, blood cascading down my leg.

Sandy grabbed my hair, jerking me backwards and slashing my back with her shard knife, ripping holes in my yoga top.

"Sandy, stop!" I tried to pull away from her, but she stabbed the arm she held in a vice-like grip. As she moved to stab me again, I reached my free arm back as far as I could, made a fist, then swung it at her jaw.

My hand writhed in pain at the resounding *crack*. Sandy stopped, her eyes rolled slightly and she crumpled to the ground.

"Mariah!" The bell over the door dinged as Maya Anderson raced into the store. She stopped when they saw me standing over Sandy, drenched in blood, which seemed to be coming out of holes all over my body.

I waved weakly, then frowned. Maya had her phone out. Was she really going to take pictures of this? "Dispatch? It's Anderson. I have an emergency at the Corner Mercantile." Maya's voice faded as she turned away.

The door flew open again as CeCe and Stormy rushed in. CeCe screamed and pointed. I followed her gaze in time to see Sandy pressing her hands beneath her shoulders to push herself up and reach for the knife shard. I kicked her in the face and she went back down.

"Sorry, Sandy."

"Do not apologize to that woman." CeCe approached us and kicked the shard away from Sandy. Stormy flew past her and landed on Sandy's back, causing the store owner to scream in pain. Stormy laid herself across Sandy's back as CeCe sat down on her legs.

"I thought you were just picking up things for Movie Night." CeCe's eyes held questions as they scanned my body to see how injured I was.

"I know, but one thing led to another."

CeCe smiled and looked around. "Mariah Stevens punched a woman, then kicked her in the face. So much for *ahimsa*."

I yawned, which surprised me. "I'm pretty sure defense of self is allowed in the yogic principles."

Maya waved her phone at me and I nodded. "Knock yourself out, Maya." She clicked away at CeCe and Stormy sitting on Sandy.

The front door banged open again and Neil rushed in. His face went white when he saw me. "Mariah, are you okay?" Without waiting for my response, he turned behind him. "Get those medics in here STAT!"

He rushed to me, donning gloves as he came. He stopped and ran his hands hovering around my body.

"Are you 'Bones' now, using your 'Star Trek' gadgets to see if I'm injured?"

He looked up into my eyes and smiled. "The snark is back. You must be okay." He surveyed my arms. "Where is all this blood coming from?"

I showed him the multitude of cuts and scratches left by Sandy's knife shard. "They sting a little, but I don't think they're serious, except this one on my thigh." I pointed to it, then raised my head toward him. "There's none on my face, right?"

His eyes searched my face before landing back on my eyes. He took my face in both of his hands. "Your face is perfect," he whispered, then softly kissed my cheek. Maya's phone clicked softly beside us. *Oh, great.*

My knees felt wobbly and it had nothing to do with my stab wounds. "I'd hug you," I whispered. "But I don't want to get you all bloody."

He smiled and pulled me gingerly into his arms. I noticed he kept the lower part of his body carefully away from my bloody legs.

Releasing me, he lifted his head and surveyed the aisle, cannisters, boxes and papers strewn across the front of the store. "I can't wait to hear the explanation of this one."

Chapter 23

Of course, Sandy went to jail. She was held without bail while waiting for her trial for second-degree murder. Her daughter came back to town and took over the store. I haven't had a chance to talk with her, because my injuries have had me hobbling somewhat, but I've seen her hauling bags of trash from the shop. CeCe said she's really cleaned up and thrown out a lot of the stuff that has been sitting on the shelves for years.

I scanned my studio, nearly crammed with friends, students and visitors.

Angelica hovered in the doorway, waiting to help Tamara. I touched her shoulder.

"In spite of everything that has happened, are you glad you came home for a while? I hear you usually only get to come home for a couple of days at a time."

"It's true. Between school and work, I don't have much free time. It feels good, though, seeing everyone and walking the old streets."

"Enough to make you want to move back here after you graduate?"

Angelica laughed, her head dipping to her chest as if embarrassed. Then she held up a hand as if to stop the questions. "I can't commit on that one yet. I really love the company I'm interning with in L.A. and it's been great working for Tamara." She leaned in closer to me. " This is my last event for her. I gave my notice last night."

She opened her arms and I reached in for a hug. She held on to me long and hard, stinging my cuts and scrapes. I winced and she released me. "Sorry, Mariah, I forgot you are still healing. Anyway, it just felt like the right time to move on, after everything that had happened."

I pulled back and held her at arm's length. "You'll still be doing yoga, though, right?"

"Definitely. In fact, I'm thinking of getting certified to teach."

"Me, too!" Stormy chimed in as she waltzed out of the office.

The smile on my face was huge and real as I wrapped my arms around both of them. "That's awesome, you guys."

Stormy broke away to attend to a confused-looking student when a familiar voice leaned in beside us.

"I know we just met last week and it hasn't gone all that well," Neil began, "but I have it from a reliable source that your big sister would like nothing better than for you to move back to Jasper. I think she kind of misses you."

Angelica hesitated, then looked Neil in the eye. "Maybe," was all she said before turning away toward the workshop.

"Not another one," Neil sighed.

I looked at him over my shoulder. "Not another what?"

"Another person in Jasper who is mad at me for doing my job."

I wanted to tell him how much it hurt to be arrested and that Angelica was likely feeling the same way toward him. But that little speech could wait. I slipped my arm around him.

"Staying for the workshop, detective?" I asked.

He rolled his eyes and shook his head.

"How about lunch later this week?"

Neil tilted his head toward me, a twinkle in his blue-gray eyes. "Perhaps Stormy and the gang can come with us?"

Oh.

I frowned and sputtered. "Actually, I was thinking just the two of us. Maybe. If that's okay with you, maybe?"

Neil's face broke into a big smile as he laughed. "I'd like nothing better, Ms. Stevens."

The tension left my body and my face broke into a big smile I couldn't seem to control. I punched him lightly on the shoulder. "You were just messing with me, weren't you?"

He smiled again, then motioned for me to follow him outside to one of the benches. I gingerly sat down on the edge, straightening out the leg where Sandy had sliced my thigh. The stitches and bandages made it a little bulky.

Neil stretched out his legs beside mine and laid his arms on the bench behind us.

"You heard Sandy is in jail, I suppose. She confessed to everything, except slashing your tires. Any idea who did that?" Neil scanned my face as he waited for my answer.

"Actually, I do." I sat back a little further on the bench. "Jennifer Parks. She was mad that I was trying to get Angelica off, so she tried to distract me. She also confessed what she had done to Maya Anderson, which is why she showed up so quickly."

The surprise was evident on Neil's face. "Why didn't you tell me? I can charge her with a misdemeanor destruction of property."

I shook my head. "No, she came to me and told me what she had done. She gave me a stack of bills to pay me back for the cost of the tires. Plus, she still wants The Yoga Mat to hold another fundraiser for Safety Blanket. So we're good."

"Wow. That's wild."

"Apparently, she'd been trying to get Jerry into a twelve-step program for years. He was in and out. That's why he wanted to make amends to Tamara. It's one of the steps they're supposed to do to stay sober."

Neil nodded. "Yeah, I got that much from Sandy. She thought Tamara would take advantage of Jerry and destroy their reputation."

I leaned my head back on the edge of the bench and looked at the sky. "I feel so bad for what happened to Angelica and Tamara with Jerry."

"There seem to be others as well." Neil smiled gently at me. "We're going to be putting out information for others so they can get therapy or whatever other kind of help they need. In fact, Tamara is setting up a fund to help them."

A smile broke across my face. "That's amazing. Now I feel bad that I thought Tamara was a killer."

Neil laughed with me. "Don't worry. It happens." He cocked an eyebrow at me pointedly. "Hopefully, they forgive you at some point."

His eyes were so blue I thought I might fall in. Instead I cleared my throat and looked down the street.

Stormy stuck her head outside the studio. "Mariah, we're ready to start."

Neil helped me to my feet and I wobbled back into the studio. My injuries made it unlikely I could do much of the class, but I wanted to welcome Tamara publicly to the studio and then listen from my office.

I turned toward Neil and impulsively kissed him on the cheek. We smiled at each other, then I slipped inside. The door softly closed behind me. I slipped off my sandals, took a deep breath and stepped into the studio.

"My friends, join me in welcoming The Goddess Tamara."

Tamara turned toward me from her place on the mat and bowed.

Namaste.

About the author

When Jacqueline M. Green first heard of "cozy mysteries," she thought her sister had brilliantly made up the term. She was delighted to discover it was a genre all its own, with tons of stories about crafting, quilting, knitting and cooking, but alas, few about yoga. As a writer, yoga instructor and lover of mysteries, she decided to solve that problem or at least add to the yoga cozies in the world. She lives with her family plus two cats, a dog and now two parakeets named Carlos and Romeo.

What's next for Mariah?

Stay tuned for *Warrior, Well Dead*, Book 3 in The Yoga Mat Cozy Mystery Series, available soon.